TEEN TITANS GO!™

MY LITTLE MUSTACHE AND FAMILY PLAN

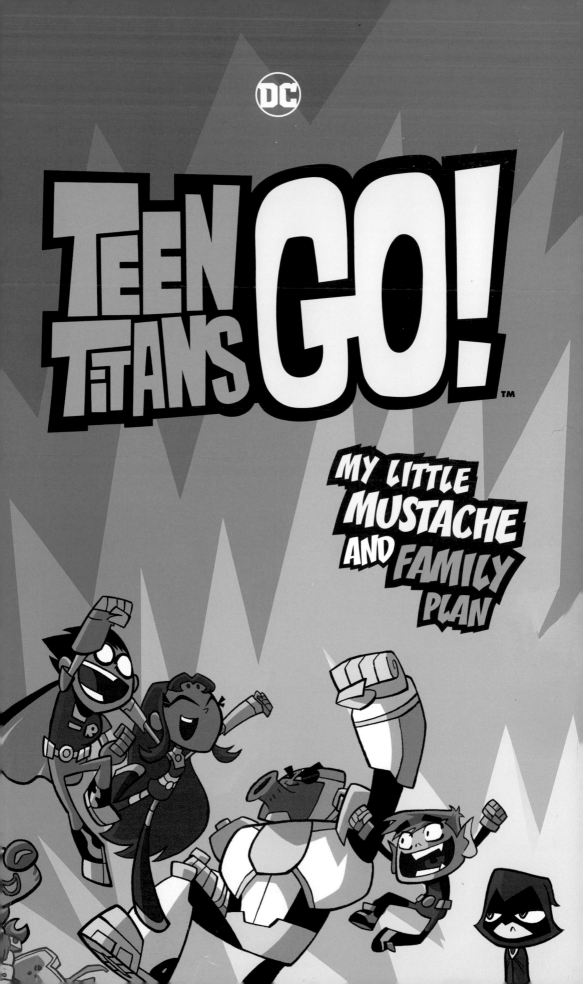

Teen Titans Go! is published by
Stone Arch Books, an imprint of Capstone.
1710 Roe Crest Drive
North Mankato, MN 56003
www.capstonepub.com

Library of Congress Cataloging-in-Publication Data is available at the Library of Congress website.
ISBN: 978-1-4965-9943-8 (library binding)
ISBN: 978-1-4965-9947-6 (eBook PDF)

Summary: It's a proud day for Cyborg when he grows his very first mustache. But what happens when said
mustache evolves into a living being and aims to turn Cyborg into . . . an adult?! Then, you think your family is
tough? Well, say hello to Raven's uncles, Horrace the Horrid, Barry the Beastly, and Myron the Mildly Irritating!

Alex Antone, Editor – Original Series

STONE ARCH BOOKS
Eliza Leahy, Editor
Kyle Grenz, Designer
Hilary Wacholz, Art Director
Kathy McColley, Production Specialist

Printed and bound in the USA.
PA117

TEEN TITANS GO!™

MERRILL HAGAN SHOLLY FISCH
WRITERS

JEREMY LAWSON DARIO BRIZUELA
ARTISTS

JEREMY LAWSON
COLORIST

WES ABBOTT
LETTERER

DAN HIPP
COVER ARTIST

STONE ARCH BOOKS
a capstone imprint

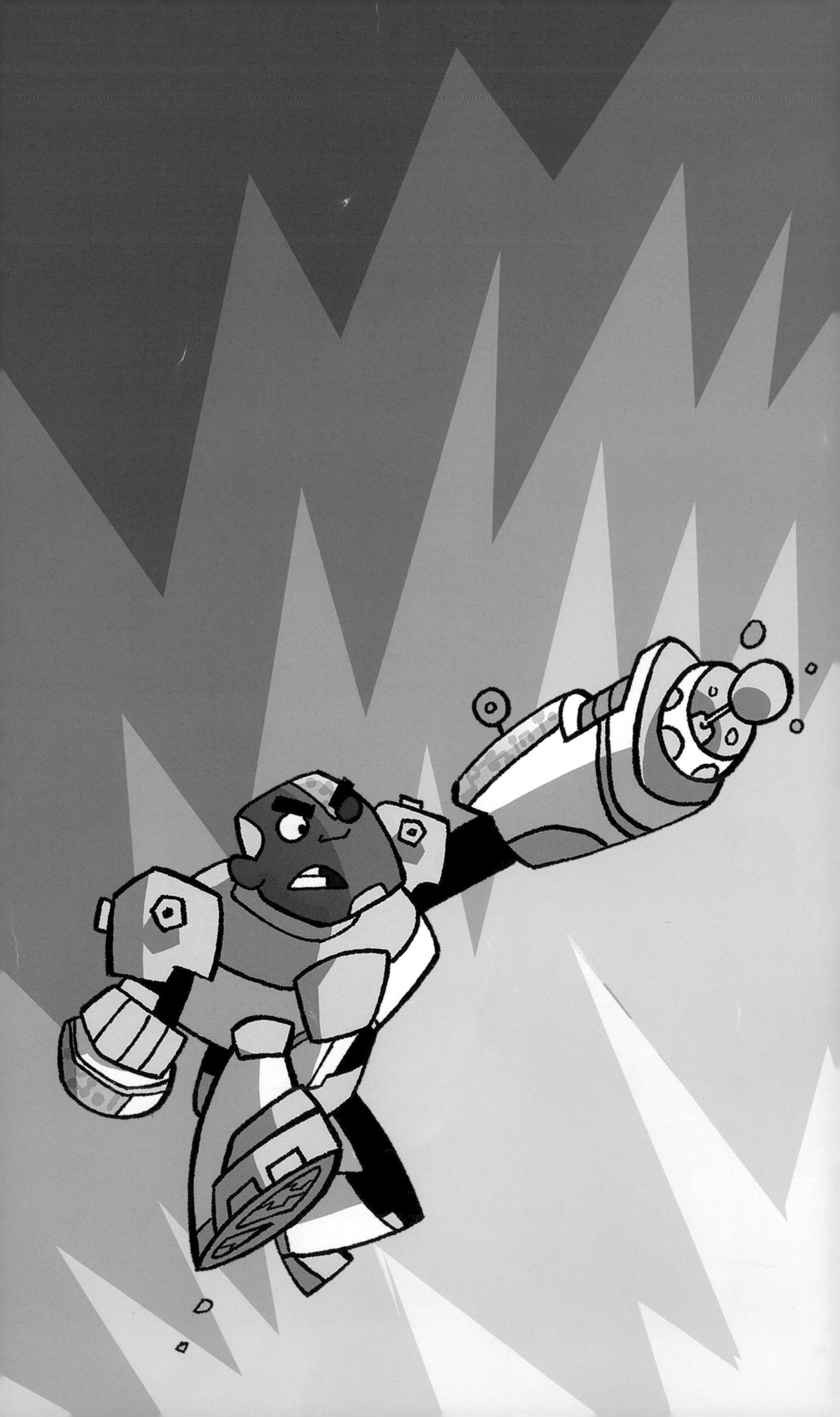

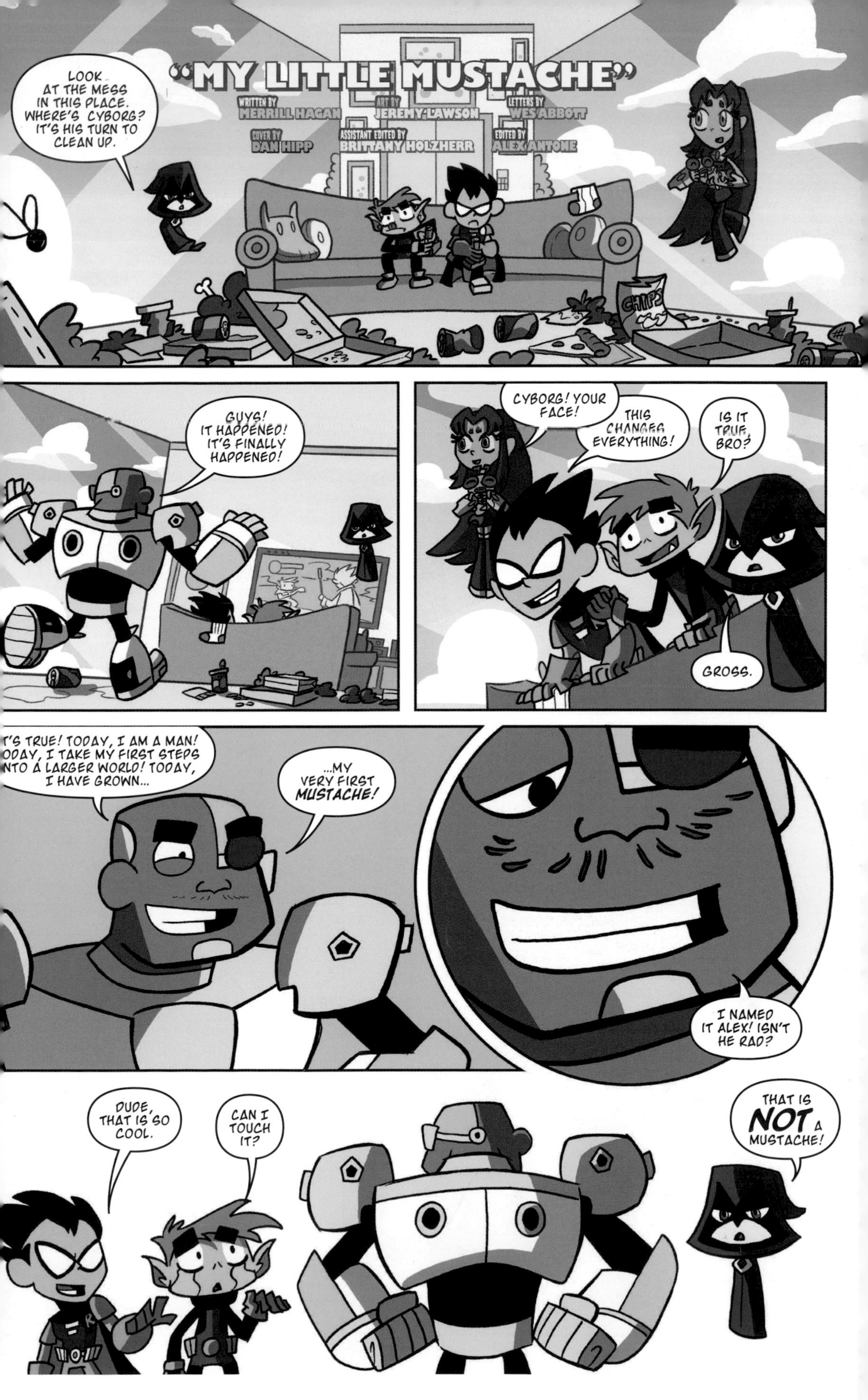
"MY LITTLE MUSTACHE"
WRITTEN BY MERRILL HAGAN
ART BY JEREMY LAWSON
LETTERS BY WES ABBOTT
COVER BY DAN HIPP
ASSISTANT EDITED BY BRITTANY HOLZHERR
EDITED BY ALEX ANTONE
LOOK AT THE MESS IN THIS PLACE. WHERE'S CYBORG? IT'S HIS TURN TO CLEAN UP.
CHIPS
GUYS! IT HAPPENED! IT'S FINALLY HAPPENED!
CYBORG! YOUR FACE!
THIS CHANGES EVERYTHING!
IS IT TRUE, BRO?
GROSS.
IT'S TRUE! TODAY, I AM A MAN! TODAY, I TAKE MY FIRST STEPS INTO A LARGER WORLD! TODAY, I HAVE GROWN...
...MY VERY FIRST MUSTACHE!
I NAMED IT ALEX! ISN'T HE RAD?
DUDE, THAT IS SO COOL.
CAN I TOUCH IT?
THAT IS NOT A MUSTACHE!

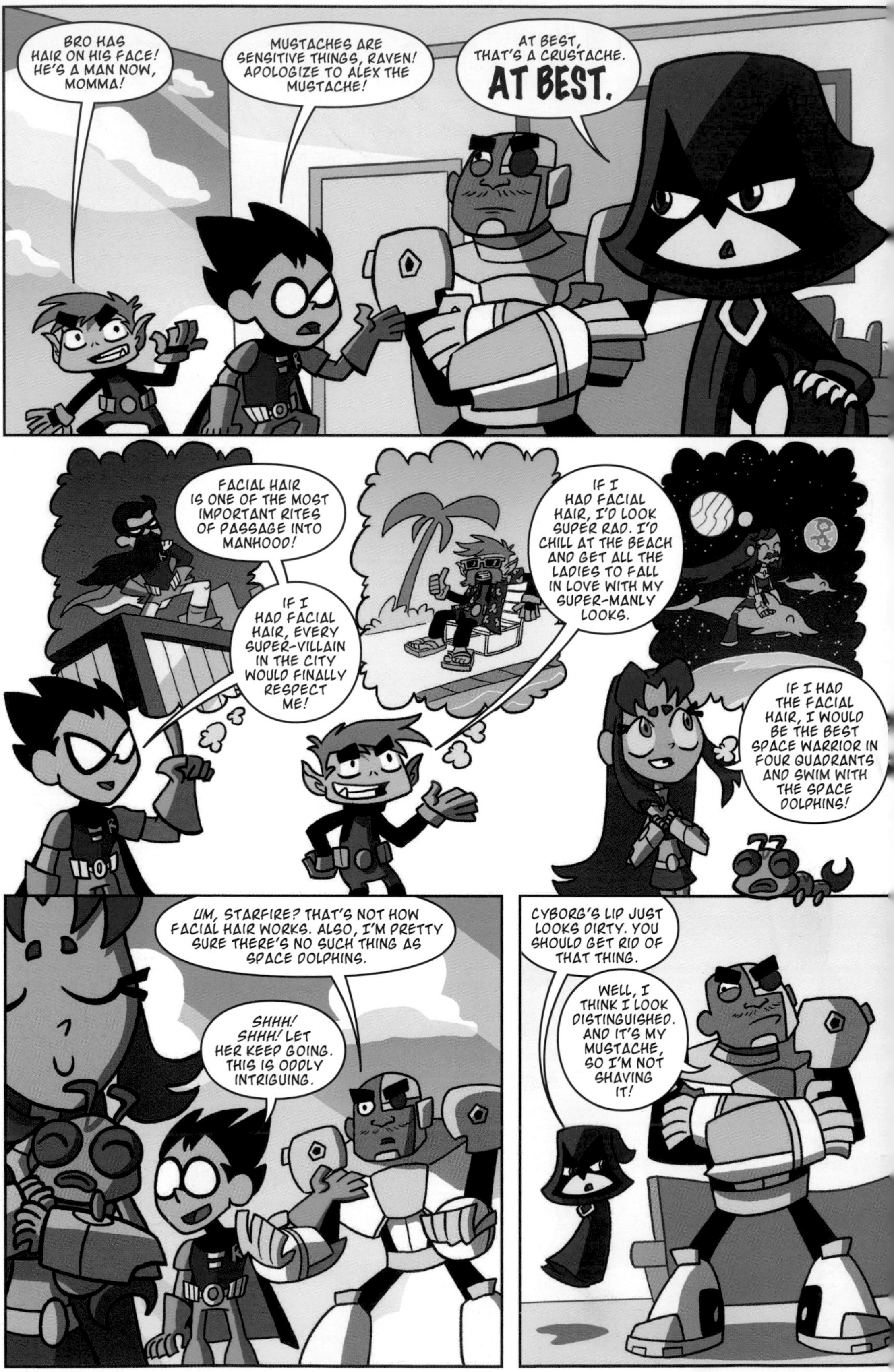
BRO HAS HAIR ON HIS FACE! HE'S A MAN NOW, MOMMA!
MUSTACHES ARE SENSITIVE THINGS, RAVEN! APOLOGIZE TO ALEX THE MUSTACHE!
AT BEST, THAT'S A CRUSTACHE. AT BEST.
FACIAL HAIR IS ONE OF THE MOST IMPORTANT RITES OF PASSAGE INTO MANHOOD!
IF I HAD FACIAL HAIR, EVERY SUPER-VILLAIN IN THE CITY WOULD FINALLY RESPECT ME!
IF I HAD FACIAL HAIR, I'D LOOK SUPER RAD. I'D CHILL AT THE BEACH AND GET ALL THE LADIES TO FALL IN LOVE WITH MY SUPER-MANLY LOOKS.
IF I HAD THE FACIAL HAIR, I WOULD BE THE BEST SPACE WARRIOR IN FOUR QUADRANTS AND SWIM WITH THE SPACE DOLPHINS!
UM, STARFIRE? THAT'S NOT HOW FACIAL HAIR WORKS. ALSO, I'M PRETTY SURE THERE'S NO SUCH THING AS SPACE DOLPHINS.
SHHH! SHHH! LET HER KEEP GOING. THIS IS ODDLY INTRIGUING.
CYBORG'S LIP JUST LOOKS DIRTY. YOU SHOULD GET RID OF THAT THING.
WELL, I THINK I LOOK DISTINGUISHED. AND IT'S MY MUSTACHE, SO I'M NOT SHAVING IT!

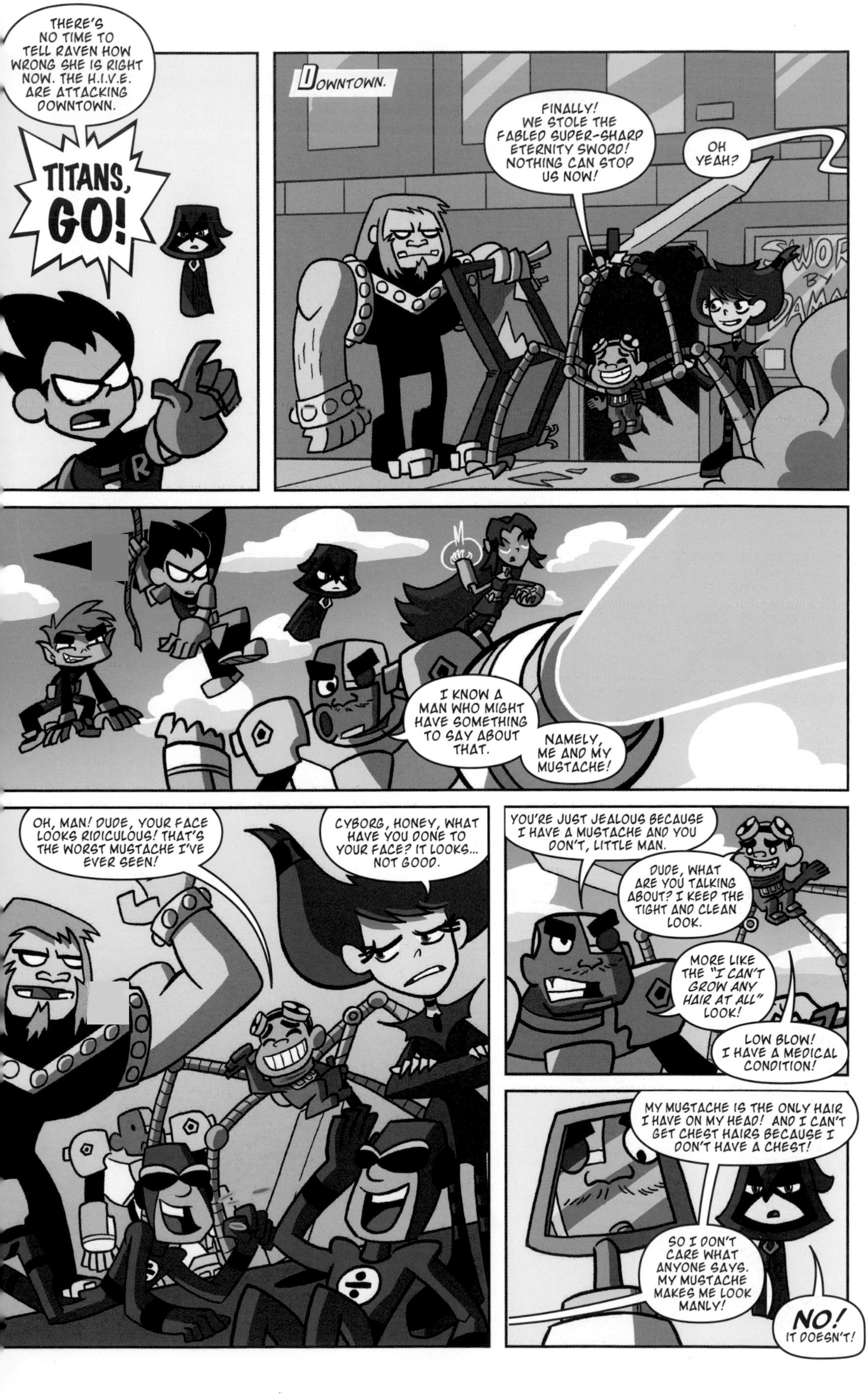

THERE'S NO TIME TO TELL RAVEN HOW WRONG SHE IS RIGHT NOW. THE H.I.V.E. ARE ATTACKING DOWNTOWN.
TITANS, GO!
DOWNTOWN.
FINALLY! WE STOLE THE FABLED SUPER-SHARP ETERNITY SWORD! NOTHING CAN STOP US NOW!
OH YEAH?
I KNOW A MAN WHO MIGHT HAVE SOMETHING TO SAY ABOUT THAT.
NAMELY, ME AND MY MUSTACHE!
OH, MAN! DUDE, YOUR FACE LOOKS RIDICULOUS! THAT'S THE WORST MUSTACHE I'VE EVER SEEN!
CYBORG, HONEY, WHAT HAVE YOU DONE TO YOUR FACE? IT LOOKS... NOT GOOD.
YOU'RE JUST JEALOUS BECAUSE I HAVE A MUSTACHE AND YOU DON'T, LITTLE MAN.
DUDE, WHAT ARE YOU TALKING ABOUT? I KEEP THE TIGHT AND CLEAN LOOK.
MORE LIKE THE "I CAN'T GROW ANY HAIR AT ALL" LOOK!
LOW BLOW! I HAVE A MEDICAL CONDITION!
MY MUSTACHE IS THE ONLY HAIR I HAVE ON MY HEAD! AND I CAN'T GET CHEST HAIRS BECAUSE I DON'T HAVE A CHEST!
SO I DON'T CARE WHAT ANYONE SAYS. MY MUSTACHE MAKES ME LOOK MANLY!
NO! IT DOESN'T!

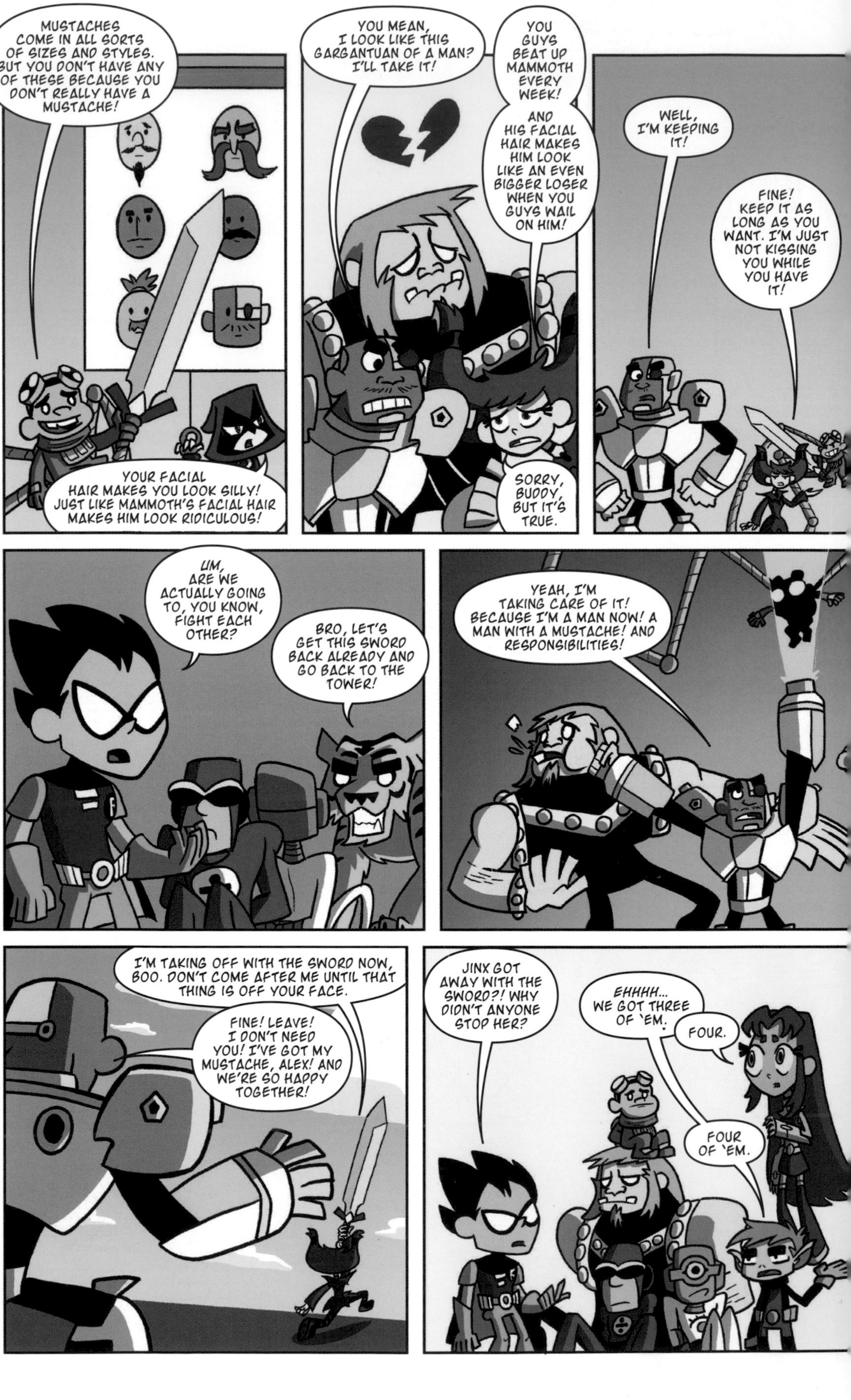

MUSTACHES COME IN ALL SORTS OF SIZES AND STYLES. BUT YOU DON'T HAVE ANY OF THESE BECAUSE YOU DON'T REALLY HAVE A MUSTACHE!
YOUR FACIAL HAIR MAKES YOU LOOK SILLY! JUST LIKE MAMMOTH'S FACIAL HAIR MAKES HIM LOOK RIDICULOUS!
YOU MEAN, I LOOK LIKE THIS GARGANTUAN OF A MAN? I'LL TAKE IT!
YOU GUYS BEAT UP MAMMOTH EVERY WEEK!
AND HIS FACIAL HAIR MAKES HIM LOOK LIKE AN EVEN BIGGER LOSER WHEN YOU GUYS WAIL ON HIM!
SORRY, BUDDY, BUT IT'S TRUE.
WELL, I'M KEEPING IT!
FINE! KEEP IT AS LONG AS YOU WANT. I'M JUST NOT KISSING YOU WHILE YOU HAVE IT!
UM, ARE WE ACTUALLY GOING TO, YOU KNOW, FIGHT EACH OTHER?
BRO, LET'S GET THIS SWORD BACK ALREADY AND GO BACK TO THE TOWER!
YEAH, I'M TAKING CARE OF IT! BECAUSE I'M A MAN NOW! A MAN WITH A MUSTACHE! AND RESPONSIBILITIES!
I'M TAKING OFF WITH THE SWORD NOW, BOO. DON'T COME AFTER ME UNTIL THAT THING IS OFF YOUR FACE.
FINE! LEAVE! I DON'T NEED YOU! I'VE GOT MY MUSTACHE, ALEX! AND WE'RE SO HAPPY TOGETHER!
JINX GOT AWAY WITH THE SWORD?! WHY DIDN'T ANYONE STOP HER?
EHHHH... WE GOT THREE OF 'EM.
FOUR.
FOUR OF 'EM.

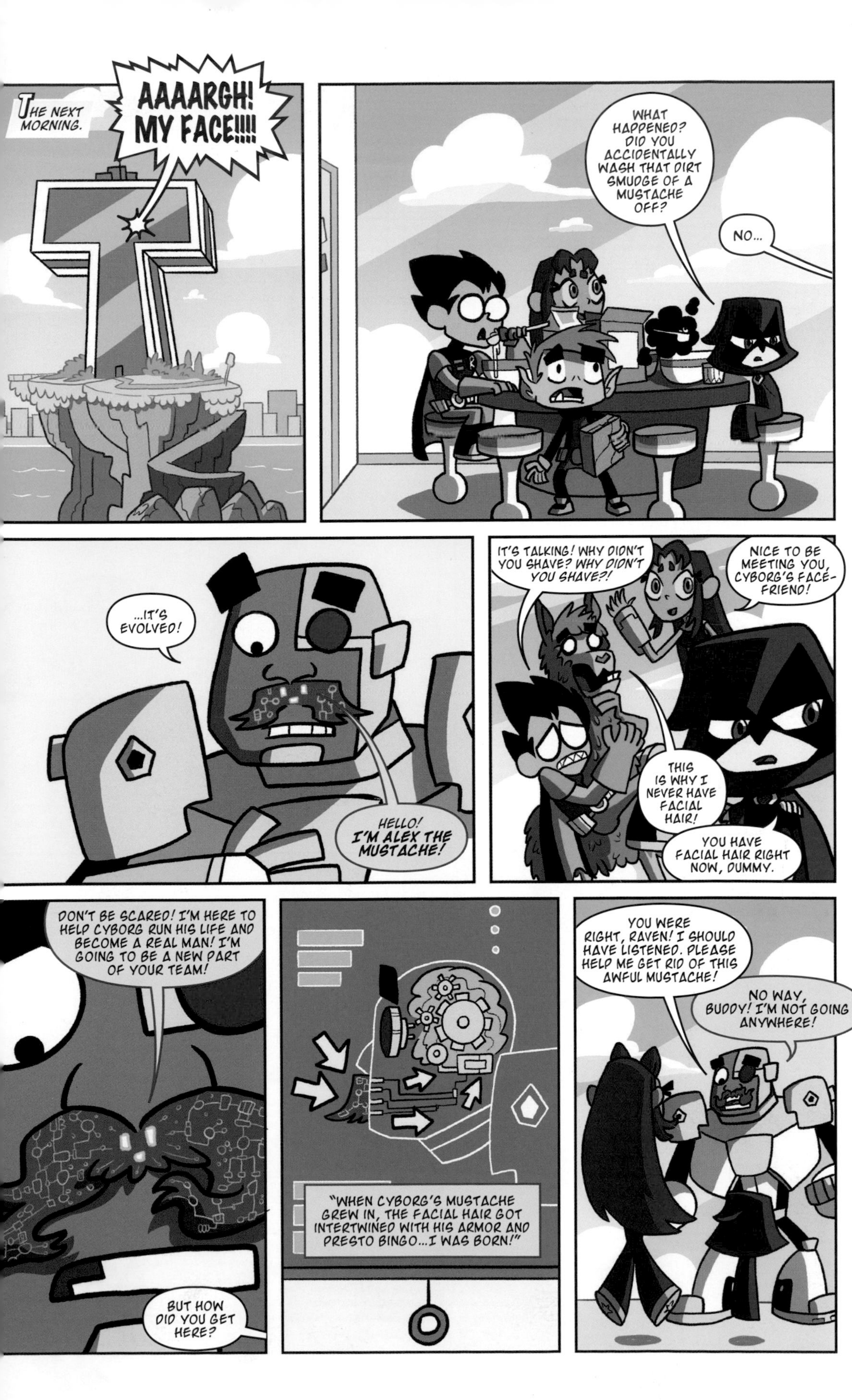

THE NEXT MORNING.
AAAARGH! MY FACE!!!!
WHAT HAPPENED? DID YOU ACCIDENTALLY WASH THAT DIRT SMUDGE OF A MUSTACHE OFF?
NO...
...IT'S EVOLVED!
HELLO! I'M ALEX THE MUSTACHE!
IT'S TALKING! WHY DIDN'T YOU SHAVE? WHY DIDN'T YOU SHAVE?!
NICE TO BE MEETING YOU, CYBORG'S FACE-FRIEND!
THIS IS WHY I NEVER HAVE FACIAL HAIR!
YOU HAVE FACIAL HAIR RIGHT NOW, DUMMY.
DON'T BE SCARED! I'M HERE TO HELP CYBORG RUN HIS LIFE AND BECOME A REAL MAN! I'M GOING TO BE A NEW PART OF YOUR TEAM!
BUT HOW DID YOU GET HERE?
"WHEN CYBORG'S MUSTACHE GREW IN, THE FACIAL HAIR GOT INTERTWINED WITH HIS ARMOR AND PRESTO BINGO...I WAS BORN!"
YOU WERE RIGHT, RAVEN! I SHOULD HAVE LISTENED. PLEASE HELP ME GET RID OF THIS AWFUL MUSTACHE!
NO WAY, BUDDY! I'M NOT GOING ANYWHERE!

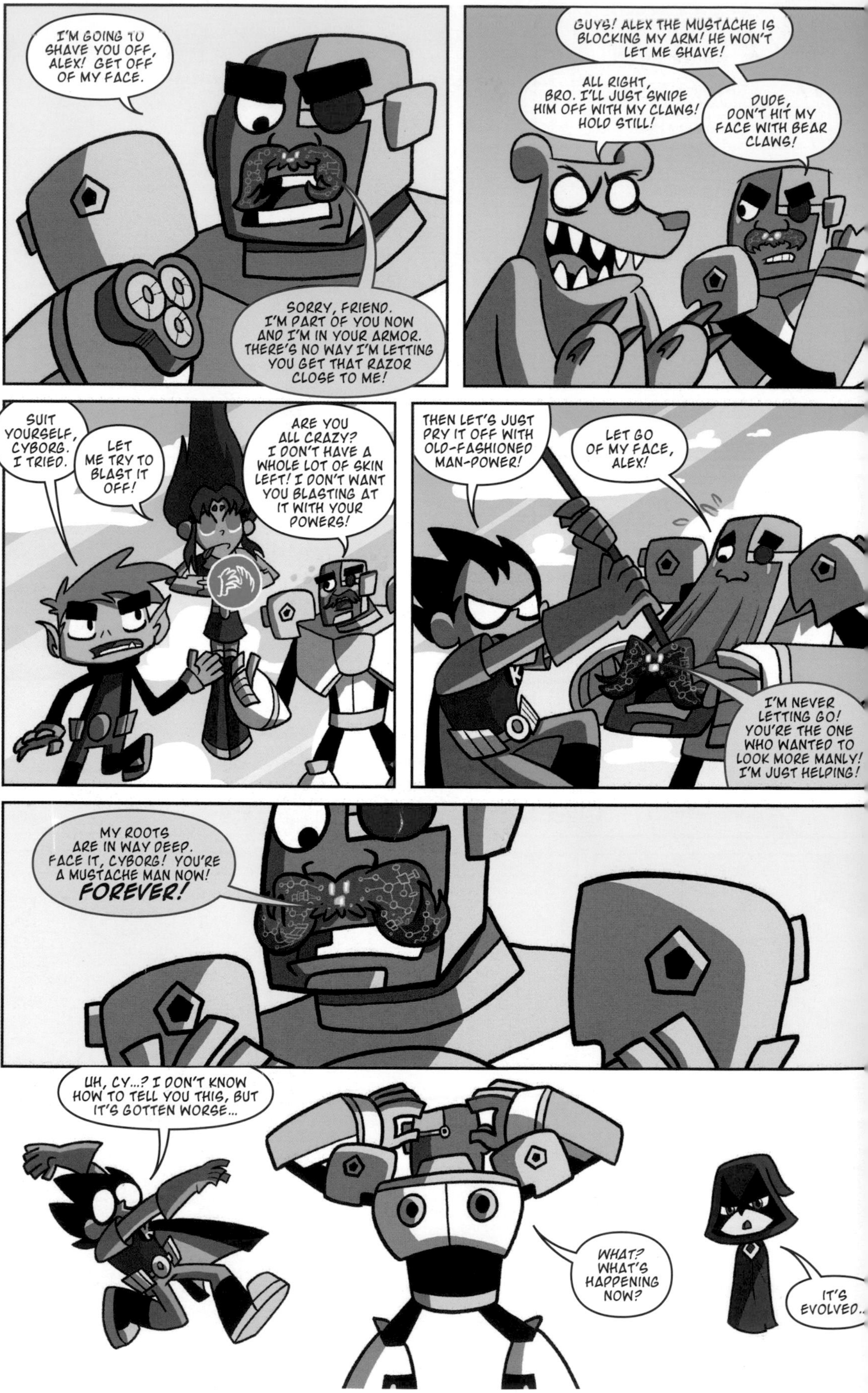
I'M GOING TO SHAVE YOU OFF, ALEX! GET OFF OF MY FACE.
SORRY, FRIEND. I'M PART OF YOU NOW AND I'M IN YOUR ARMOR. THERE'S NO WAY I'M LETTING YOU GET THAT RAZOR CLOSE TO ME!
GUYS! ALEX THE MUSTACHE IS BLOCKING MY ARM! HE WON'T LET ME SHAVE!
ALL RIGHT, BRO. I'LL JUST SWIPE HIM OFF WITH MY CLAWS! HOLD STILL!
DUDE, DON'T HIT MY FACE WITH BEAR CLAWS!
SUIT YOURSELF, CYBORG. I TRIED.
LET ME TRY TO BLAST IT OFF!
ARE YOU ALL CRAZY? I DON'T HAVE A WHOLE LOT OF SKIN LEFT! I DON'T WANT YOU BLASTING AT IT WITH YOUR POWERS!
THEN LET'S JUST PRY IT OFF WITH OLD-FASHIONED MAN-POWER!
LET GO OF MY FACE, ALEX!
I'M NEVER LETTING GO! YOU'RE THE ONE WHO WANTED TO LOOK MORE MANLY! I'M JUST HELPING!
MY ROOTS ARE IN WAY DEEP. FACE IT, CYBORG! YOU'RE A MUSTACHE MAN NOW! FOREVER!
UH, CY...? I DON'T KNOW HOW TO TELL YOU THIS, BUT IT'S GOTTEN WORSE...
WHAT? WHAT'S HAPPENING NOW?
IT'S EVOLVED...

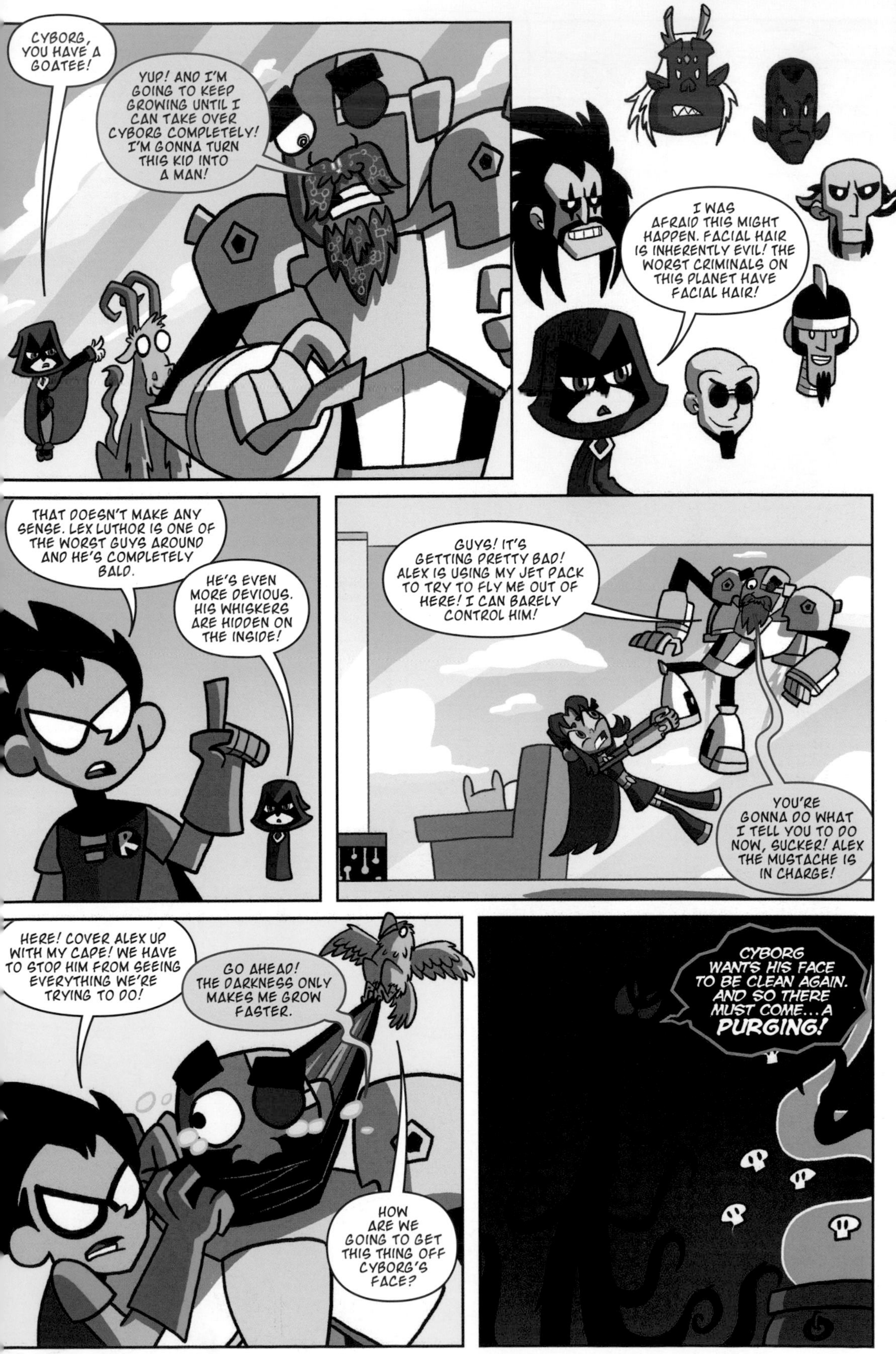
CYBORG, YOU HAVE A GOATEE!
YUP! AND I'M GOING TO KEEP GROWING UNTIL I CAN TAKE OVER CYBORG COMPLETELY! I'M GONNA TURN THIS KID INTO A MAN!
I WAS AFRAID THIS MIGHT HAPPEN. FACIAL HAIR IS INHERENTLY EVIL! THE WORST CRIMINALS ON THIS PLANET HAVE FACIAL HAIR!
THAT DOESN'T MAKE ANY SENSE. LEX LUTHOR IS ONE OF THE WORST GUYS AROUND AND HE'S COMPLETELY BALD.
HE'S EVEN MORE DEVIOUS. HIS WHISKERS ARE HIDDEN ON THE INSIDE!
GUYS! IT'S GETTING PRETTY BAD! ALEX IS USING MY JET PACK TO TRY TO FLY ME OUT OF HERE! I CAN BARELY CONTROL HIM!
YOU'RE GONNA DO WHAT I TELL YOU TO DO NOW, SUCKER! ALEX THE MUSTACHE IS IN CHARGE!
HERE! COVER ALEX UP WITH MY CAPE! WE HAVE TO STOP HIM FROM SEEING EVERYTHING WE'RE TRYING TO DO!
GO AHEAD! THE DARKNESS ONLY MAKES ME GROW FASTER.
HOW ARE WE GOING TO GET THIS THING OFF CYBORG'S FACE?
CYBORG WANTS HIS FACE TO BE CLEAN AGAIN. AND SO THERE MUST COME... A PURGING!

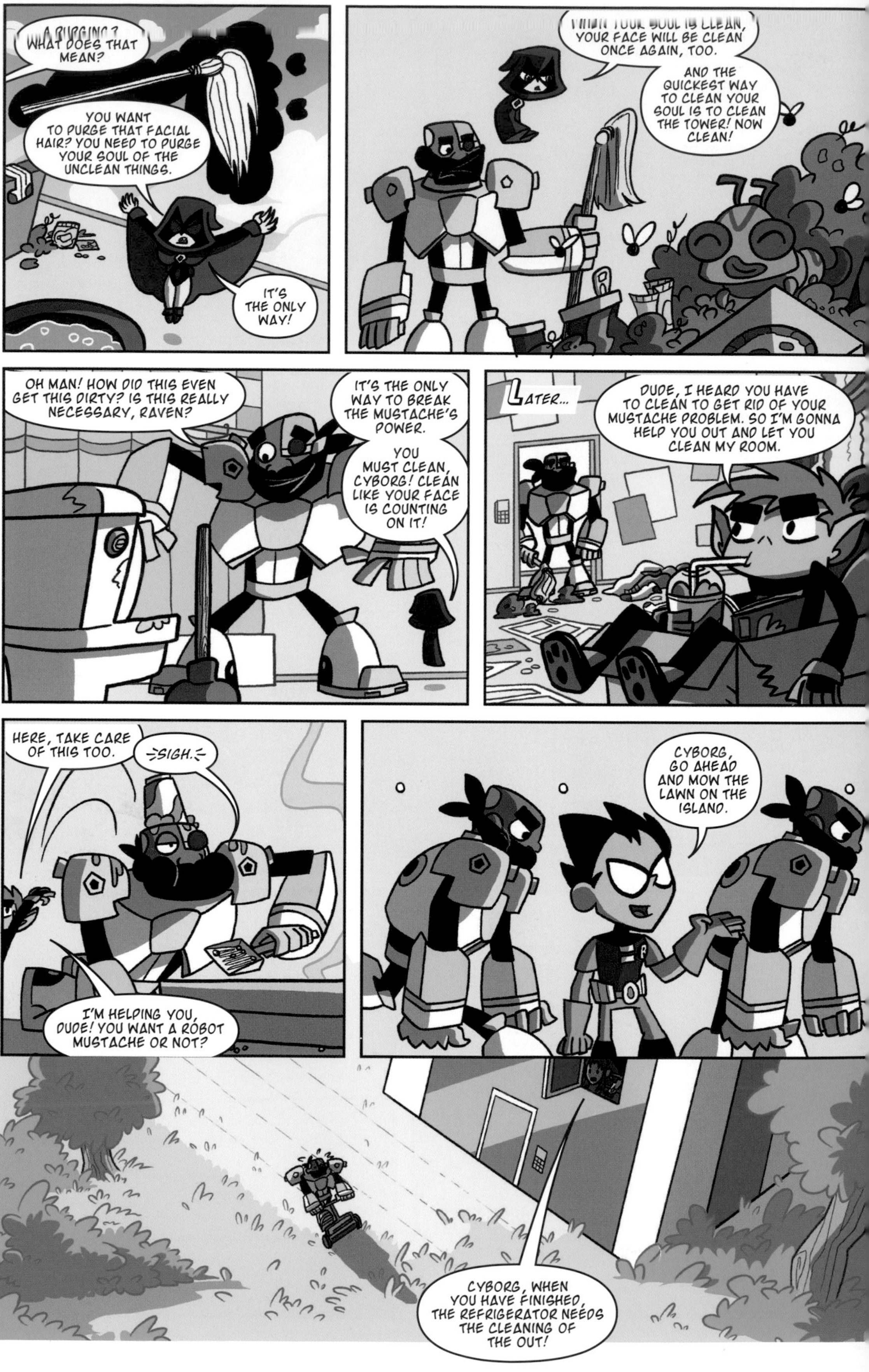
A PURGING? WHAT DOES THAT MEAN?
YOU WANT TO PURGE THAT FACIAL HAIR? YOU NEED TO PURGE YOUR SOUL OF THE UNCLEAN THINGS.
IT'S THE ONLY WAY!
WHEN YOUR SOUL IS CLEAN, YOUR FACE WILL BE CLEAN ONCE AGAIN, TOO.
AND THE QUICKEST WAY TO CLEAN YOUR SOUL IS TO CLEAN THE TOWER! NOW CLEAN!
OH MAN! HOW DID THIS EVEN GET THIS DIRTY? IS THIS REALLY NECESSARY, RAVEN?
IT'S THE ONLY WAY TO BREAK THE MUSTACHE'S POWER.
YOU MUST CLEAN, CYBORG! CLEAN LIKE YOUR FACE IS COUNTING ON IT!
LATER...
DUDE, I HEARD YOU HAVE TO CLEAN TO GET RID OF YOUR MUSTACHE PROBLEM. SO I'M GONNA HELP YOU OUT AND LET YOU CLEAN MY ROOM.
HERE, TAKE CARE OF THIS TOO.
SIGH.
I'M HELPING YOU, DUDE! YOU WANT A ROBOT MUSTACHE OR NOT?
CYBORG, GO AHEAD AND MOW THE LAWN ON THE ISLAND.
CYBORG, WHEN YOU HAVE FINISHED, THE REFRIGERATOR NEEDS THE CLEANING OF THE OUT!

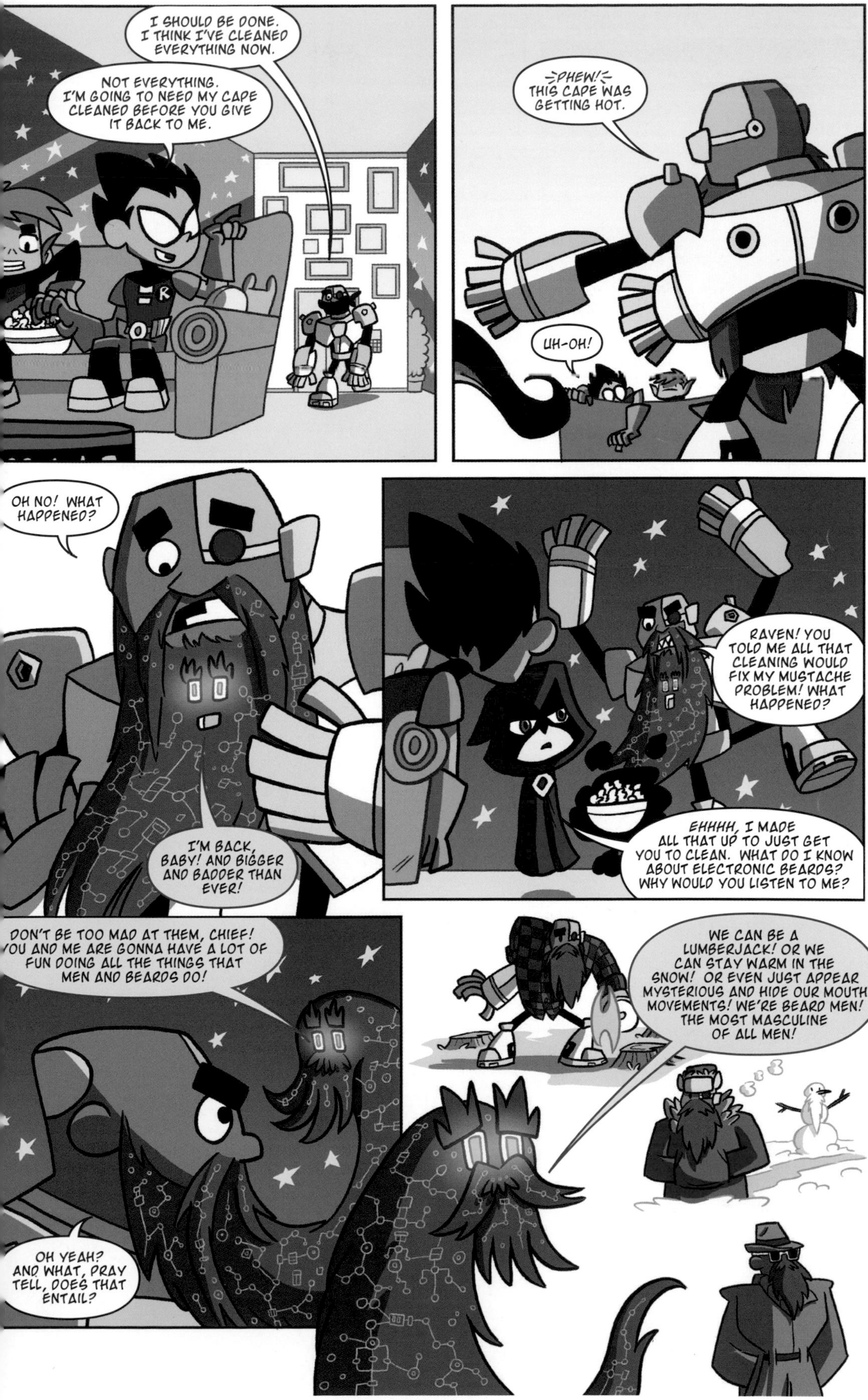
I SHOULD BE DONE. I THINK I'VE CLEANED EVERYTHING NOW.
NOT EVERYTHING. I'M GOING TO NEED MY CAPE CLEANED BEFORE YOU GIVE IT BACK TO ME.
PHEW! THIS CAPE WAS GETTING HOT.
UH-OH!
OH NO! WHAT HAPPENED?
I'M BACK, BABY! AND BIGGER AND BADDER THAN EVER!
RAVEN! YOU TOLD ME ALL THAT CLEANING WOULD FIX MY MUSTACHE PROBLEM! WHAT HAPPENED?
EHHHH, I MADE ALL THAT UP TO JUST GET YOU TO CLEAN. WHAT DO I KNOW ABOUT ELECTRONIC BEARDS? WHY WOULD YOU LISTEN TO ME?
DON'T BE TOO MAD AT THEM, CHIEF! YOU AND ME ARE GONNA HAVE A LOT OF FUN DOING ALL THE THINGS THAT MEN AND BEARDS DO!
OH YEAH? AND WHAT, PRAY TELL, DOES THAT ENTAIL?
WE CAN BE A LUMBERJACK! OR WE CAN STAY WARM IN THE SNOW! OR EVEN JUST APPEAR MYSTERIOUS AND HIDE OUR MOUTH MOVEMENTS! WE'RE BEARD MEN! THE MOST MASCULINE OF ALL MEN!

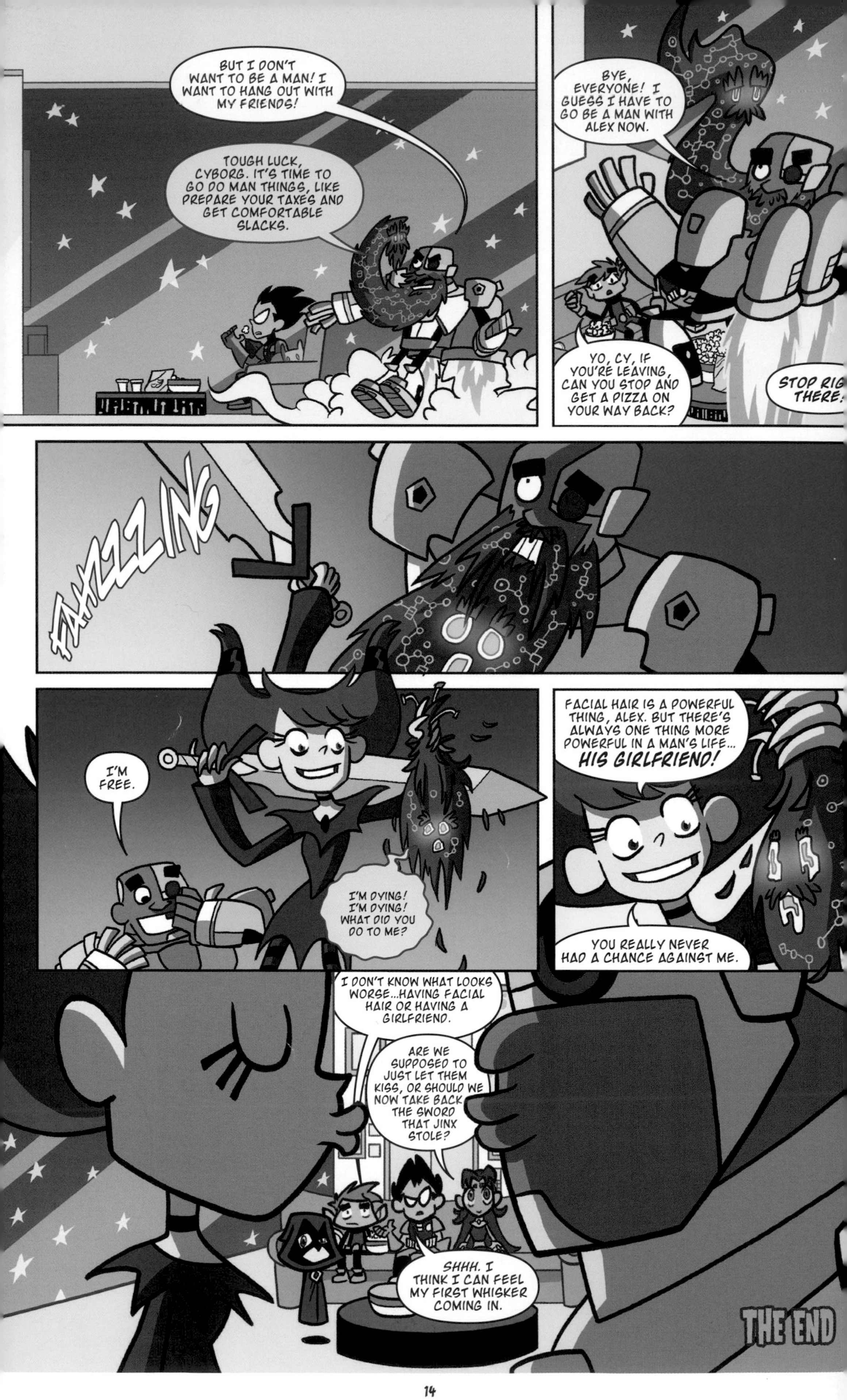

BUT I DON'T WANT TO BE A MAN! I WANT TO HANG OUT WITH MY FRIENDS!
TOUGH LUCK, CYBORG. IT'S TIME TO GO DO MAN THINGS, LIKE PREPARE YOUR TAXES AND GET COMFORTABLE SLACKS.
BYE, EVERYONE! I GUESS I HAVE TO GO BE A MAN WITH ALEX NOW.
YO, CY, IF YOU'RE LEAVING, CAN YOU STOP AND GET A PIZZA ON YOUR WAY BACK?
FAHZZZING
I'M FREE.
I'M DYING! I'M DYING! WHAT DID YOU DO TO ME?
FACIAL HAIR IS A POWERFUL THING, ALEX. BUT THERE'S ALWAYS ONE THING MORE POWERFUL IN A MAN'S LIFE... HIS GIRLFRIEND!
YOU REALLY NEVER HAD A CHANCE AGAINST ME.
I DON'T KNOW WHAT LOOKS WORSE...HAVING FACIAL HAIR OR HAVING A GIRLFRIEND.
ARE WE SUPPOSED TO JUST LET THEM KISS, OR SHOULD WE NOW TAKE BACK THE SWORD THAT JINX STOLE?
SHHH. I THINK I CAN FEEL MY FIRST WHISKER COMING IN.
THE END

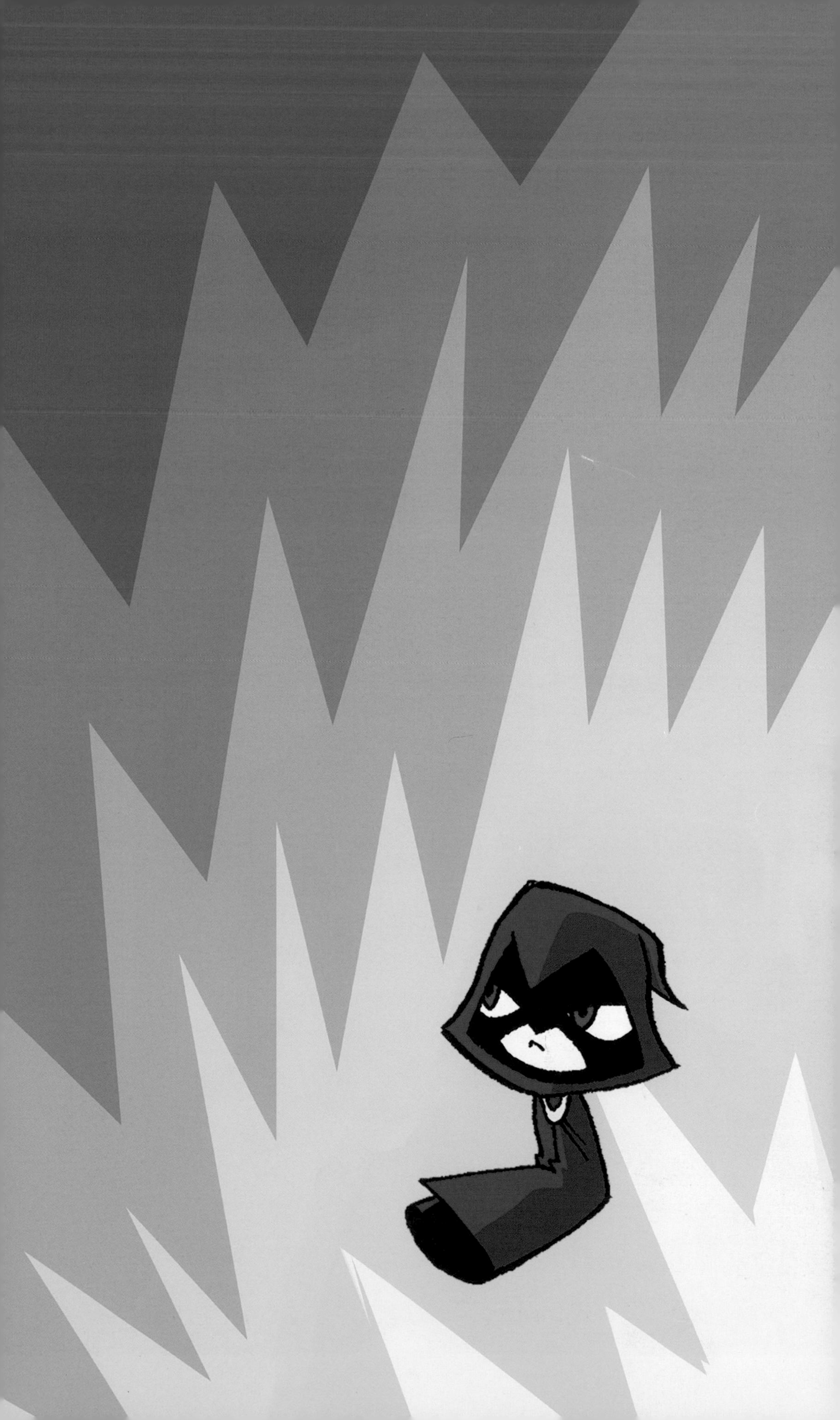

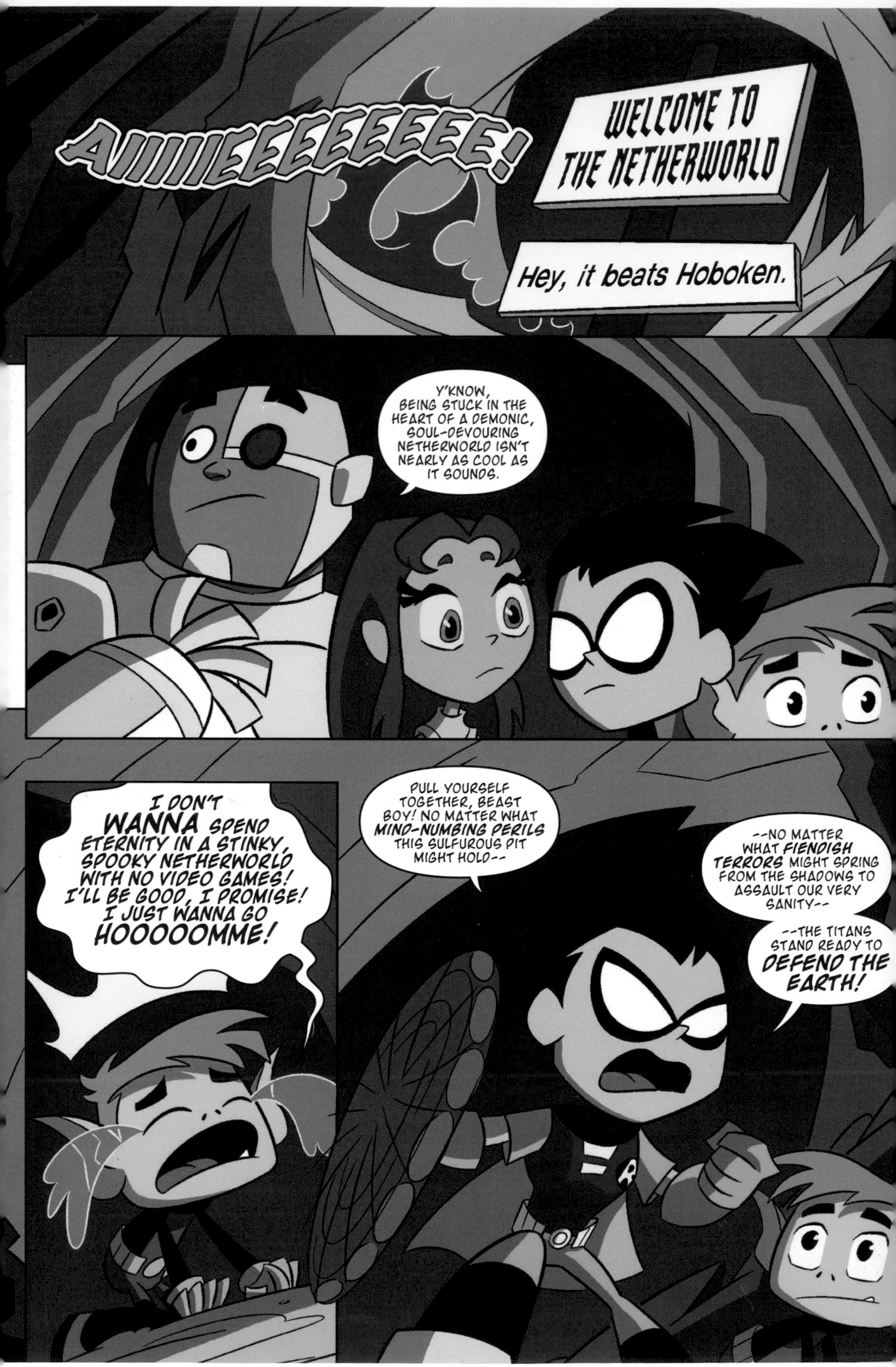
AIIIIIEEEEEEEEE!
WELCOME TO THE NETHERWORLD
Hey, it beats Hoboken.
Y'KNOW, BEING STUCK IN THE HEART OF A DEMONIC, SOUL-DEVOURING NETHERWORLD ISN'T NEARLY AS COOL AS IT SOUNDS.
I DON'T WANNA SPEND ETERNITY IN A STINKY, SPOOKY NETHERWORLD WITH NO VIDEO GAMES! I'LL BE GOOD, I PROMISE! I JUST WANNA GO HOOOOOMME!
PULL YOURSELF TOGETHER, BEAST BOY! NO MATTER WHAT MIND-NUMBING PERILS THIS SULFUROUS PIT MIGHT HOLD--
--NO MATTER WHAT FIENDISH TERRORS MIGHT SPRING FROM THE SHADOWS TO ASSAULT OUR VERY SANITY--
--THE TITANS STAND READY TO DEFEND THE EARTH!

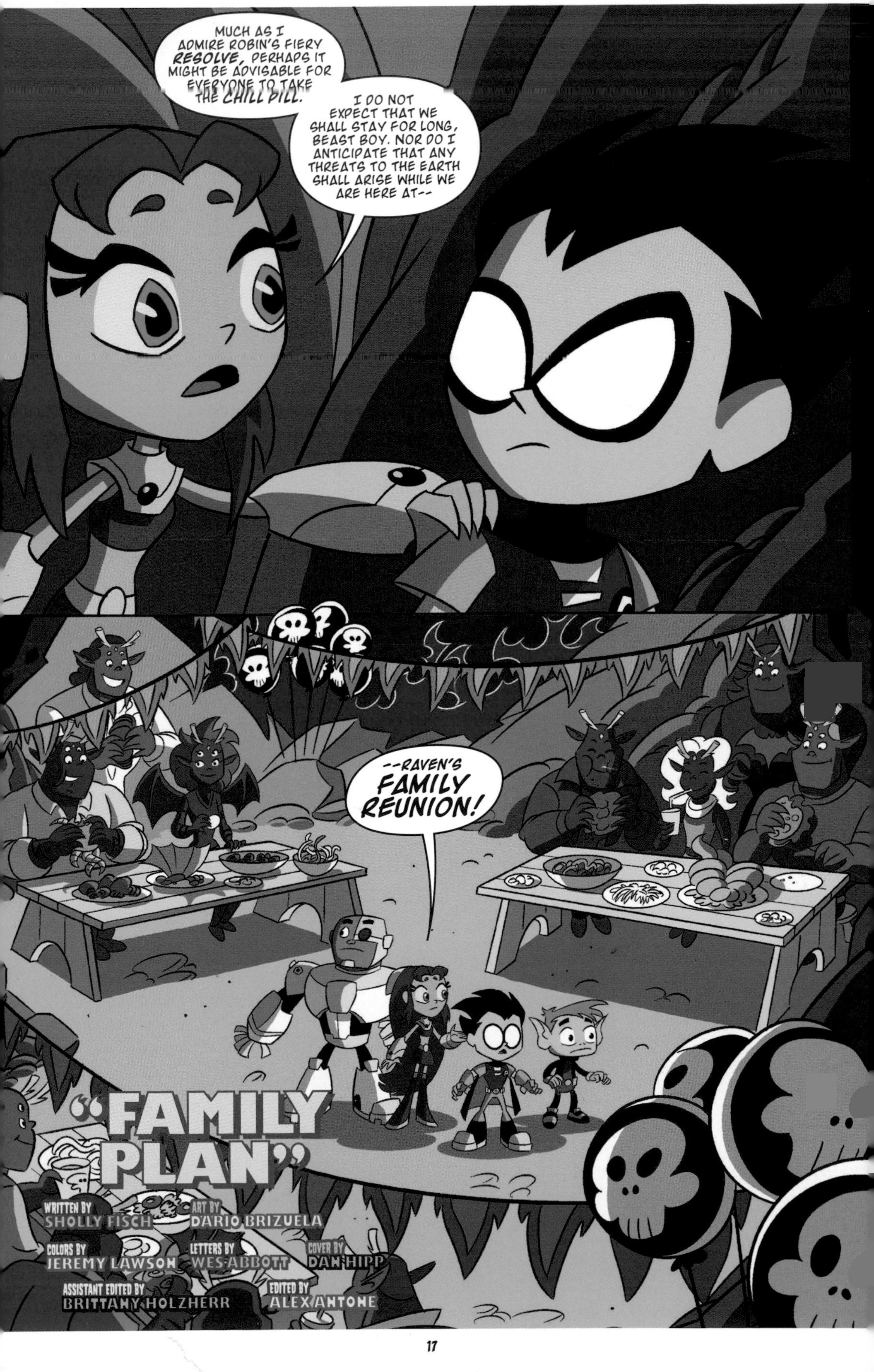
MUCH AS I ADMIRE ROBIN'S FIERY RESOLVE, PERHAPS IT MIGHT BE ADVISABLE FOR EVERYONE TO TAKE THE CHILL PILL.
I DO NOT EXPECT THAT WE SHALL STAY FOR LONG, BEAST BOY. NOR DO I ANTICIPATE THAT ANY THREATS TO THE EARTH SHALL ARISE WHILE WE ARE HERE AT--
--RAVEN'S FAMILY REUNION!
"FAMILY PLAN"
WRITTEN BY SHOLLY FISCH
ART BY DARIO BRIZUELA
COLORS BY JEREMY LAWSON
LETTERS BY WES ABBOTT
COVER BY DAN HIPP
ASSISTANT EDITED BY BRITTANY HOLZHERR
EDITED BY ALEX ANTONE

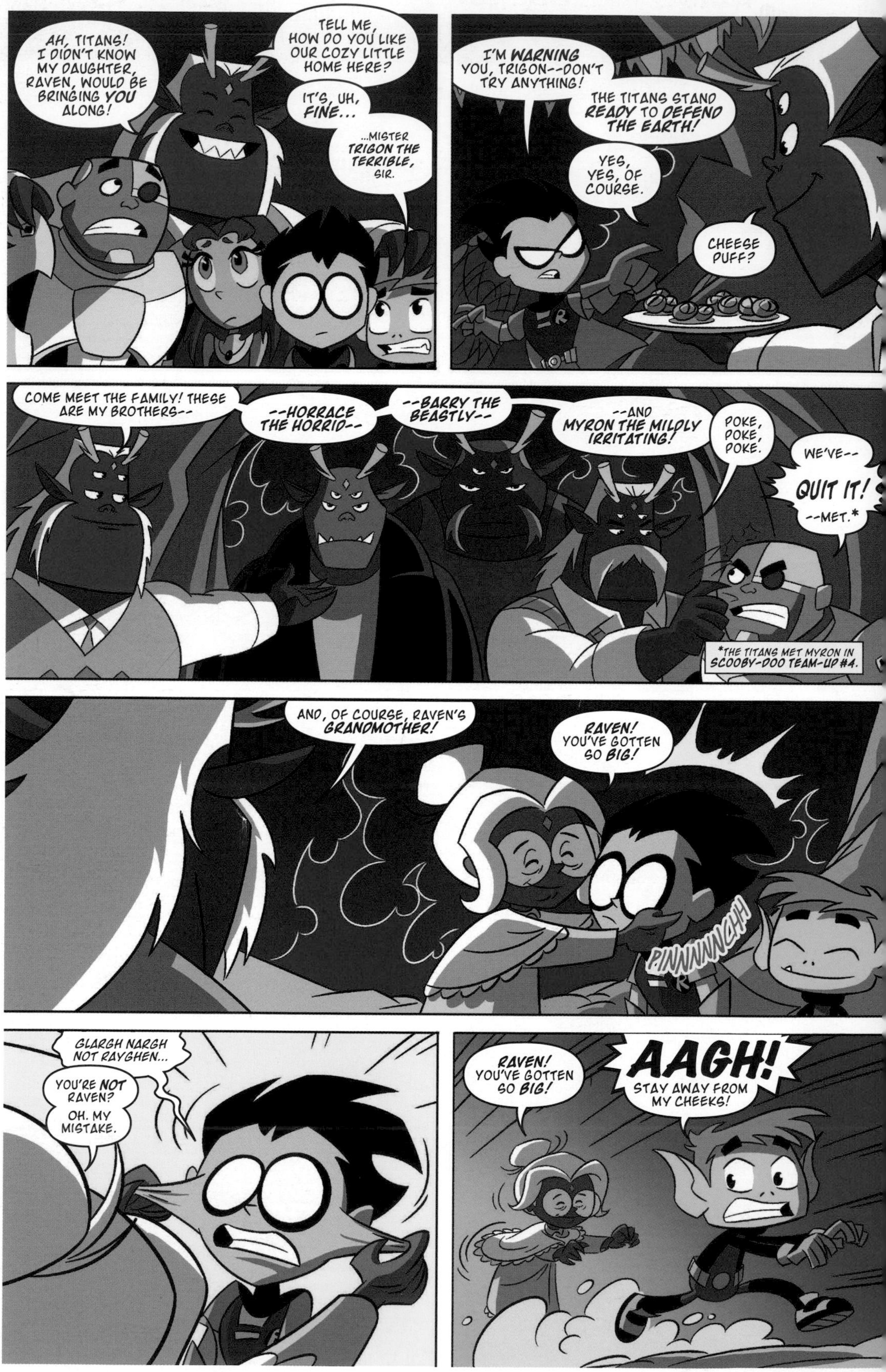
AH, TITANS! I DIDN'T KNOW MY DAUGHTER, RAVEN, WOULD BE BRINGING YOU ALONG!
TELL ME, HOW DO YOU LIKE OUR COZY LITTLE HOME HERE?
IT'S, UH, FINE...
...MISTER TRIGON THE TERRIBLE, SIR.
I'M WARNING YOU, TRIGON--DON'T TRY ANYTHING!
THE TITANS STAND READY TO DEFEND THE EARTH!
YES, YES, OF COURSE.
CHEESE PUFF?
COME MEET THE FAMILY! THESE ARE MY BROTHERS--
--HORRACE THE HORRID--
--BARRY THE BEASTLY--
--AND MYRON THE MILDLY IRRITATING!
POKE, POKE, POKE.
WE'VE--
QUIT IT!
--MET.*
*THE TITANS MET MYRON IN SCOOBY-DOO TEAM-UP #4.
AND, OF COURSE, RAVEN'S GRANDMOTHER!
RAVEN! YOU'VE GOTTEN SO BIG!
PINNNNNCHH
GLARGH NARGH NOT RAYGHEN...
YOU'RE NOT RAVEN? OH. MY MISTAKE.
RAVEN! YOU'VE GOTTEN SO BIG!
AAGH!
STAY AWAY FROM MY CHEEKS!

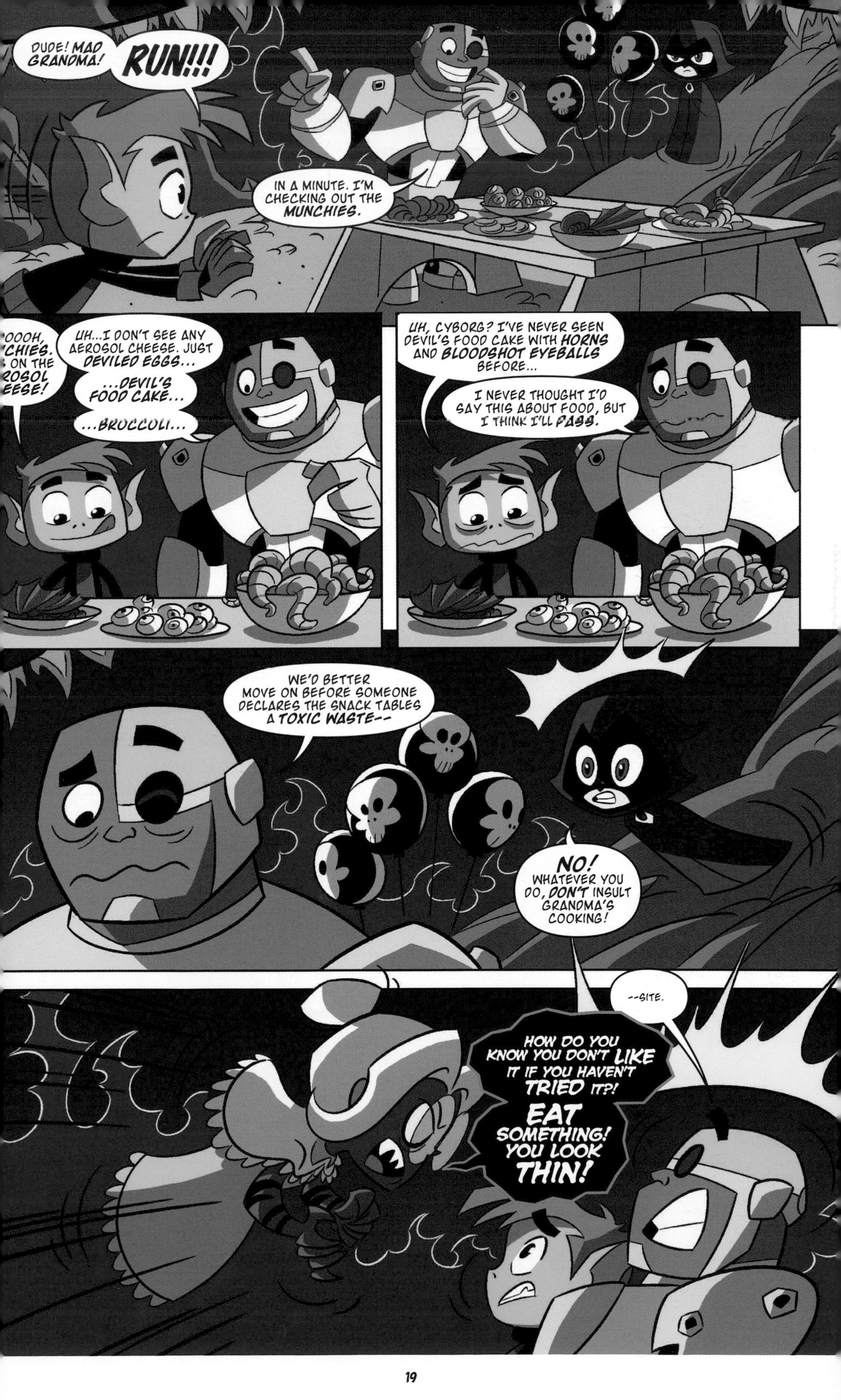
DUDE! MAD GRANDMA!
RUN!!!
IN A MINUTE. I'M CHECKING OUT THE MUNCHIES.
OOOH, ...CHIES. ... ON THE ...ROSOL ...EESE!
UH...I DON'T SEE ANY AEROSOL CHEESE. JUST DEVILED EGGS...
...DEVIL'S FOOD CAKE...
...BROCCOLI...
UH, CYBORG? I'VE NEVER SEEN DEVIL'S FOOD CAKE WITH HORNS AND BLOODSHOT EYEBALLS BEFORE...
I NEVER THOUGHT I'D SAY THIS ABOUT FOOD, BUT I THINK I'LL PASS.
WE'D BETTER MOVE ON BEFORE SOMEONE DECLARES THE SNACK TABLES A TOXIC WASTE--
NO! WHATEVER YOU DO, DON'T INSULT GRANDMA'S COOKING!
--SITE.
HOW DO YOU KNOW YOU DON'T LIKE IT IF YOU HAVEN'T TRIED IT?!
EAT SOMETHING! YOU LOOK THIN!

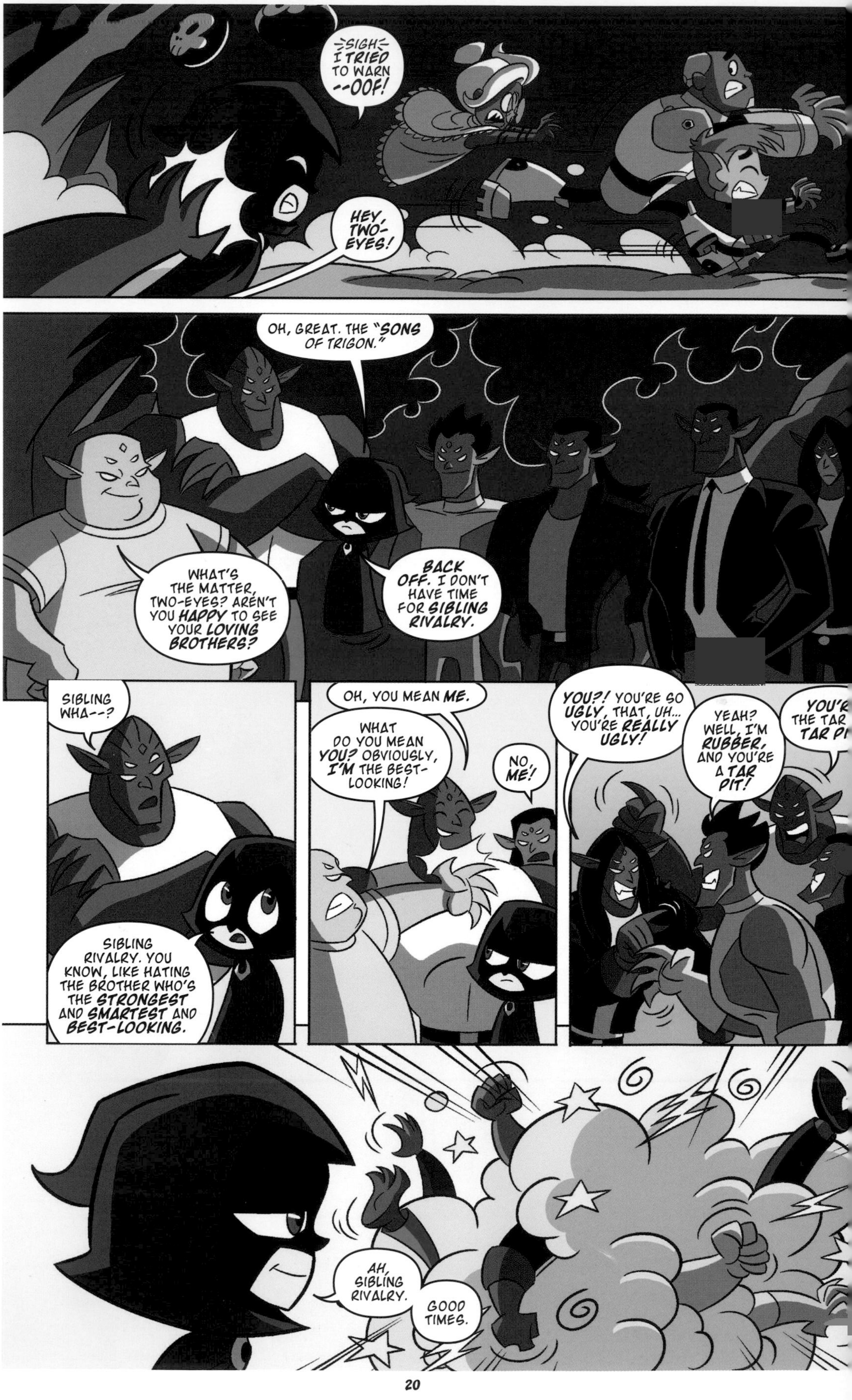
-SIGH- I TRIED TO WARN --OOF!
HEY, TWO-EYES!
OH, GREAT. THE "SONS OF TRIGON."
WHAT'S THE MATTER, TWO-EYES? AREN'T YOU HAPPY TO SEE YOUR LOVING BROTHERS?
BACK OFF. I DON'T HAVE TIME FOR SIBLING RIVALRY.
SIBLING WHA--?
SIBLING RIVALRY. YOU KNOW, LIKE HATING THE BROTHER WHO'S THE STRONGEST AND SMARTEST AND BEST-LOOKING.
OH, YOU MEAN ME.
WHAT DO YOU MEAN YOU? OBVIOUSLY, I'M THE BEST-LOOKING!
NO, ME!
YOU?! YOU'RE SO UGLY, THAT, UH... YOU'RE REALLY UGLY!
YEAH? WELL, I'M RUBBER, AND YOU'RE A TAR PIT!
YOU'R THE TAR TAR PI
AH, SIBLING RIVALRY.
GOOD TIMES.

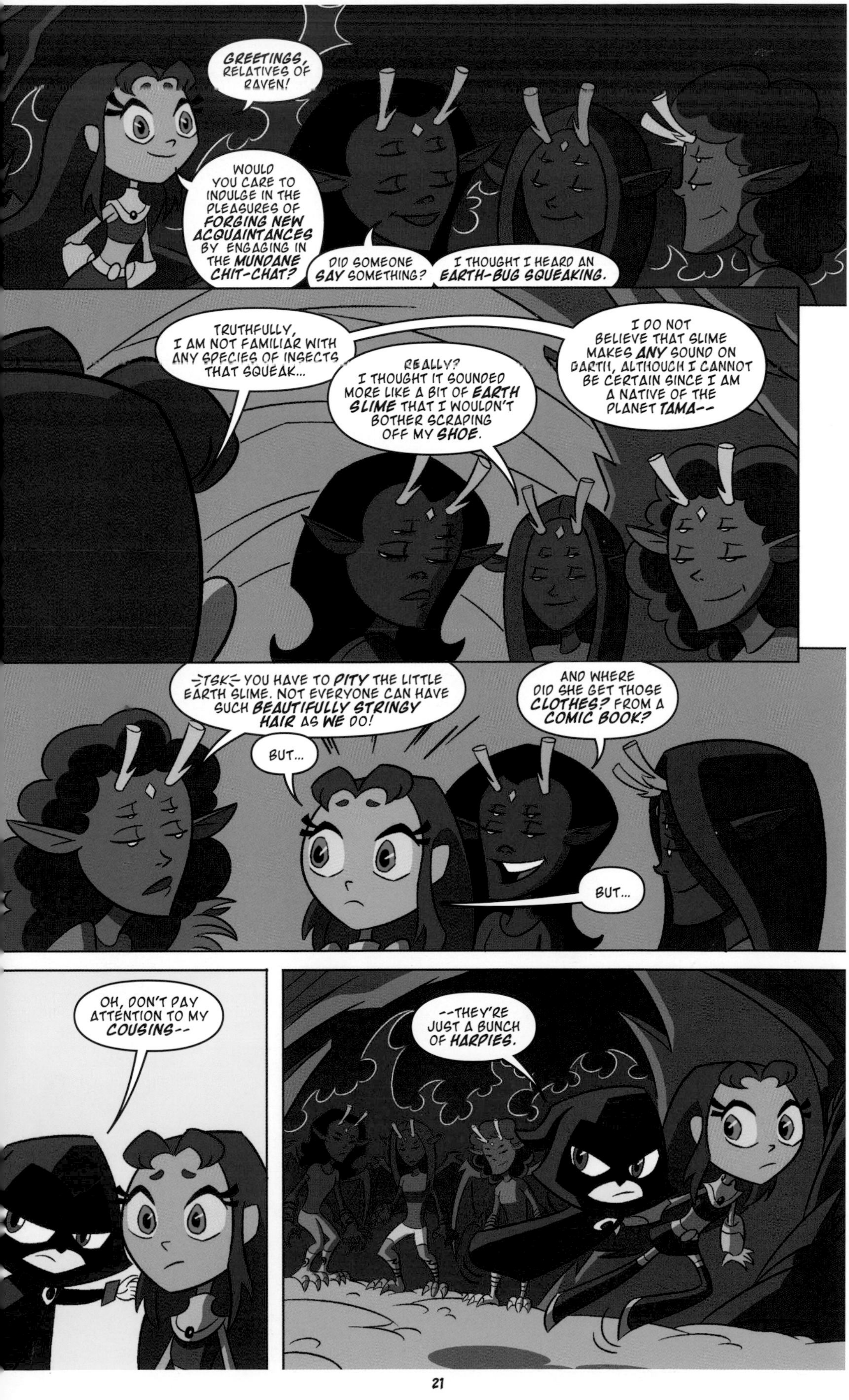
GREETINGS, RELATIVES OF RAVEN!
WOULD YOU CARE TO INDULGE IN THE PLEASURES OF FORGING NEW ACQUAINTANCES BY ENGAGING IN THE MUNDANE CHIT-CHAT?
DID SOMEONE SAY SOMETHING?
I THOUGHT I HEARD AN EARTH-BUG SQUEAKING.
TRUTHFULLY, I AM NOT FAMILIAR WITH ANY SPECIES OF INSECTS THAT SQUEAK...
REALLY? I THOUGHT IT SOUNDED MORE LIKE A BIT OF EARTH SLIME THAT I WOULDN'T BOTHER SCRAPING OFF MY SHOE.
I DO NOT BELIEVE THAT SLIME MAKES ANY SOUND ON EARTH, ALTHOUGH I CANNOT BE CERTAIN SINCE I AM A NATIVE OF THE PLANET TAMA--
TSK YOU HAVE TO PITY THE LITTLE EARTH SLIME. NOT EVERYONE CAN HAVE SUCH BEAUTIFULLY STRINGY HAIR AS WE DO!
BUT...
AND WHERE DID SHE GET THOSE CLOTHES? FROM A COMIC BOOK?
BUT...
OH, DON'T PAY ATTENTION TO MY COUSINS--
--THEY'RE JUST A BUNCH OF HARPIES.

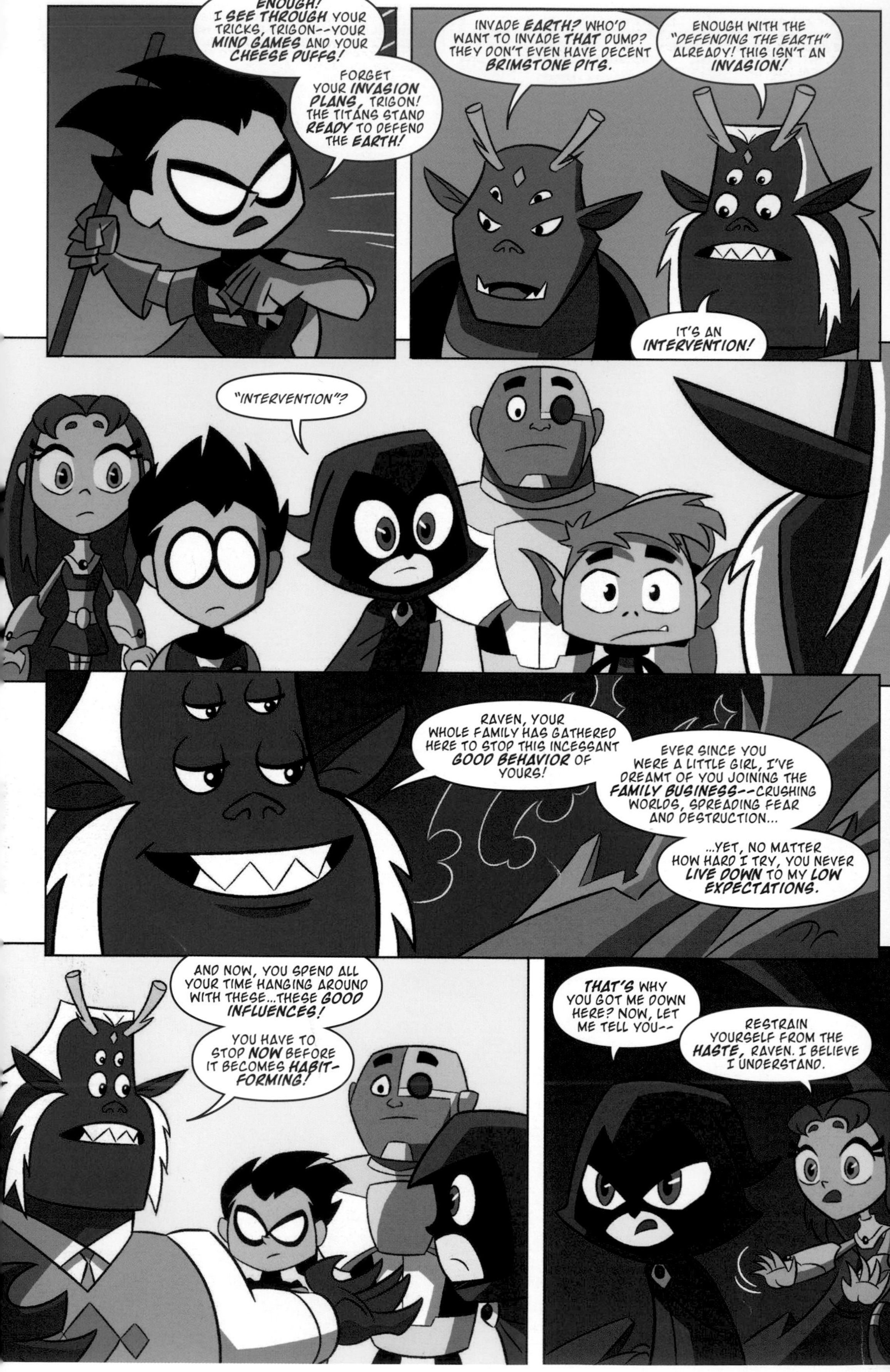

ENOUGH! I SEE THROUGH YOUR TRICKS, TRIGON--YOUR MIND GAMES AND YOUR CHEESE PUFFS!
FORGET YOUR INVASION PLANS, TRIGON! THE TITANS STAND READY TO DEFEND THE EARTH!
INVADE EARTH? WHO'D WANT TO INVADE THAT DUMP? THEY DON'T EVEN HAVE DECENT BRIMSTONE PITS.
ENOUGH WITH THE "DEFENDING THE EARTH" ALREADY! THIS ISN'T AN INVASION!
IT'S AN INTERVENTION!
"INTERVENTION"?
RAVEN, YOUR WHOLE FAMILY HAS GATHERED HERE TO STOP THIS INCESSANT GOOD BEHAVIOR OF YOURS!
EVER SINCE YOU WERE A LITTLE GIRL, I'VE DREAMT OF YOU JOINING THE FAMILY BUSINESS--CRUSHING WORLDS, SPREADING FEAR AND DESTRUCTION...
...YET, NO MATTER HOW HARD I TRY, YOU NEVER LIVE DOWN TO MY LOW EXPECTATIONS.
AND NOW, YOU SPEND ALL YOUR TIME HANGING AROUND WITH THESE...THESE GOOD INFLUENCES!
YOU HAVE TO STOP NOW BEFORE IT BECOMES HABIT-FORMING!
THAT'S WHY YOU GOT ME DOWN HERE? NOW, LET ME TELL YOU--
RESTRAIN YOURSELF FROM THE HASTE, RAVEN. I BELIEVE I UNDERSTAND.

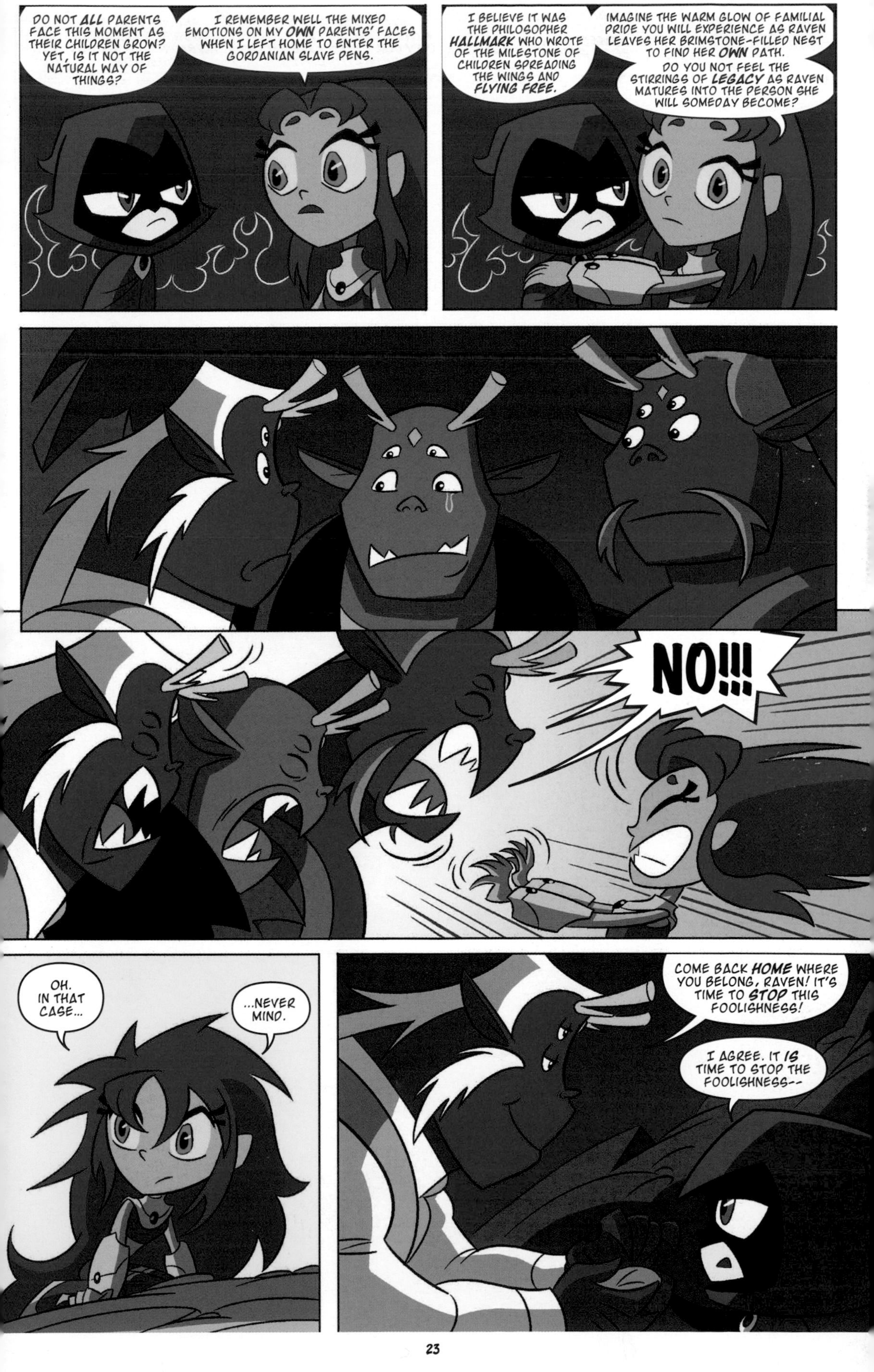
DO NOT ALL PARENTS FACE THIS MOMENT AS THEIR CHILDREN GROW? YET, IS IT NOT THE NATURAL WAY OF THINGS?
I REMEMBER WELL THE MIXED EMOTIONS ON MY OWN PARENTS' FACES WHEN I LEFT HOME TO ENTER THE GORDANIAN SLAVE PENS.
I BELIEVE IT WAS THE PHILOSOPHER HALLMARK WHO WROTE OF THE MILESTONE OF CHILDREN SPREADING THE WINGS AND FLYING FREE.
IMAGINE THE WARM GLOW OF FAMILIAL PRIDE YOU WILL EXPERIENCE AS RAVEN LEAVES HER BRIMSTONE-FILLED NEST TO FIND HER OWN PATH.
DO YOU NOT FEEL THE STIRRINGS OF LEGACY AS RAVEN MATURES INTO THE PERSON SHE WILL SOMEDAY BECOME?
NO!!!
OH. IN THAT CASE...
...NEVER MIND.
COME BACK HOME WHERE YOU BELONG, RAVEN! IT'S TIME TO STOP THIS FOOLISHNESS!
I AGREE. IT IS TIME TO STOP THE FOOLISHNESS--

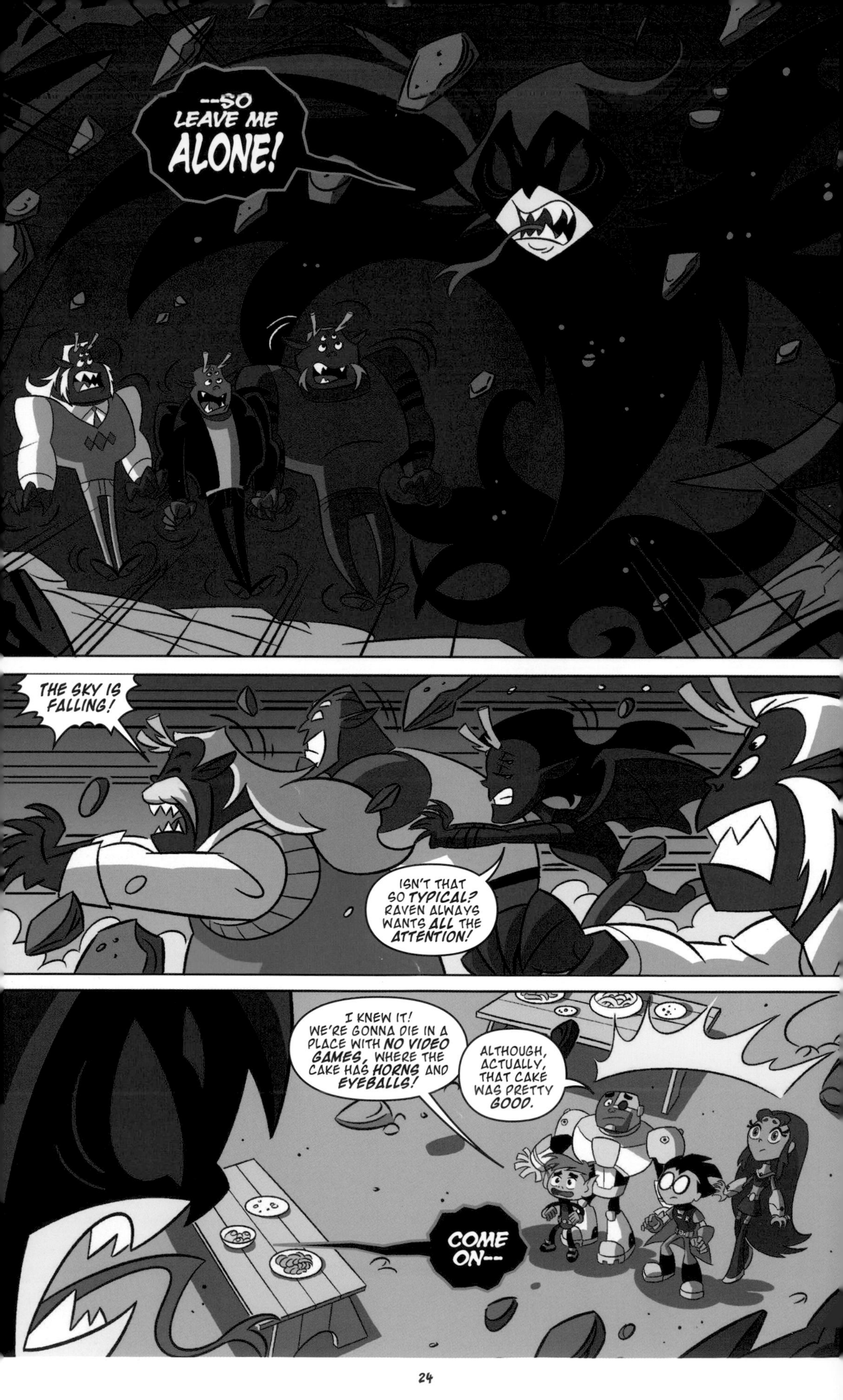

--SO LEAVE ME ALONE!
THE SKY IS FALLING!
ISN'T THAT SO TYPICAL? RAVEN ALWAYS WANTS ALL THE ATTENTION!
I KNEW IT! WE'RE GONNA DIE IN A PLACE WITH NO VIDEO GAMES, WHERE THE CAKE HAS HORNS AND EYEBALLS!
ALTHOUGH, ACTUALLY, THAT CAKE WAS PRETTY GOOD.
COME ON--

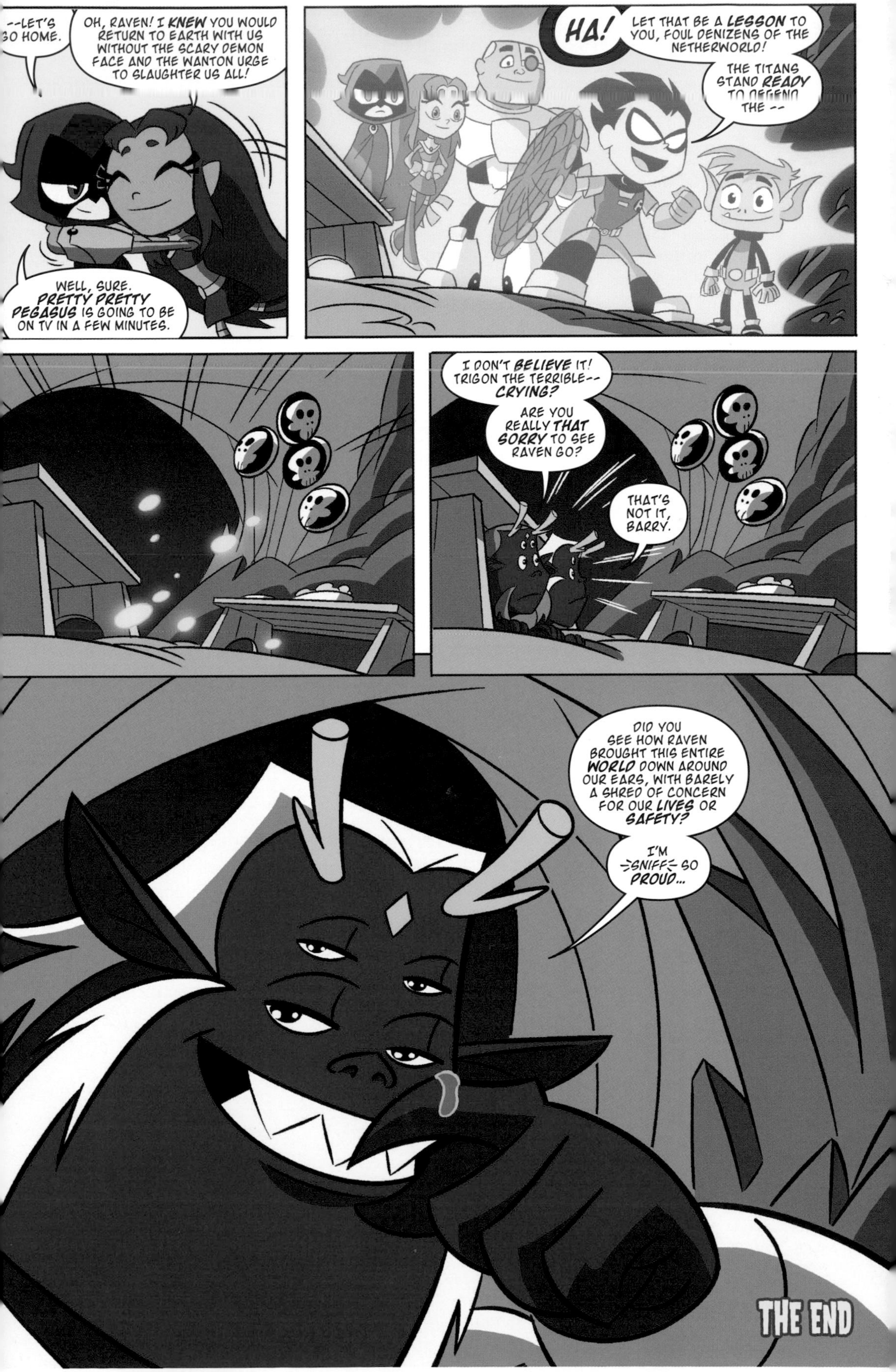

--LET'S GO HOME.
OH, RAVEN! I KNEW YOU WOULD RETURN TO EARTH WITH US WITHOUT THE SCARY DEMON FACE AND THE WANTON URGE TO SLAUGHTER US ALL!
WELL, SURE. PRETTY PRETTY PEGASUS IS GOING TO BE ON TV IN A FEW MINUTES.
HA!
LET THAT BE A LESSON TO YOU, FOUL DENIZENS OF THE NETHERWORLD!
THE TITANS STAND READY TO DEFEND THE --
I DON'T BELIEVE IT! TRIGON THE TERRIBLE--CRYING?
ARE YOU REALLY THAT SORRY TO SEE RAVEN GO?
THAT'S NOT IT, BARRY.
DID YOU SEE HOW RAVEN BROUGHT THIS ENTIRE WORLD DOWN AROUND OUR EARS, WITH BARELY A SHRED OF CONCERN FOR OUR LIVES OR SAFETY?
I'M =SNIFF= SO PROUD...
THE END

CREATORS

MERRILL HAGAN

Merrill Hagan is a writer who has worked on numerous episodes of the hit *Teen Titans Go!* TV show. In addition, he has authored several Teen Titans Go! comic books and was a writer for the original Teen Titans series in 2003.

SHOLLY FISCH

Bitten by a radioactive typewriter, Sholly Fisch has spent the wee hours writing books, comics, TV scripts, and online material for over 25 years. His comic book credits include more than 200 stories and features about characters such as Batman, Superman, Bugs Bunny, Daffy Duck, Spider-Man, and Ben 10. Currently, he writes stories for Action Comics every month, plus stories for Looney Tunes and Scooby-Doo. By day, Sholly is a mild-mannered developmental psychologist who helps to create educational TV shows, websites, and other media for kids.

JEREMY LAWSON

Jeremy Lawson is a highly caffeinated cartoonist from Texas. He now lives in Colorado, and he's getting better at making the books he wished he'd had as a kid.

DARIO BRIZUELA

Dario Brizuela was born in Buenos Aires, Argentina, in 1977. He enjoys doing illustration work and character design for several companies including DC Comics, Marvel Comics, Image Comics, IDW Publishing, Titan Publishing, Hasbro, Capstone Publishers, and Disney Publishing Worldwide. Dario's work can be found in a wide range of properties including Star Wars Tales, Ben 10, DC Super Friends, Justice League Unlimited, Batman: The Brave & The Bold, Transformers, Teenage Mutant Ninja Turtles, Batman 66, Wonder Woman 77, Teen Titans Go!, Scooby-Doo! Team Up, and DC Super Hero Girls.

GLOSSARY

acquaintance (uh-KWAYN-tuhns)—someone you have met but do not know well

anticipate (an-TIS-uh-pate)—to expect something to happen and be prepared for it

bloodshot (BLUHD-shaht)—red and irritated

denizen (DEN-uh-zuhn)—a person who lives or is often found in a place

eternity (ih-TUR-ni-tee)—a seemingly endless amount of time

gargantuan (gahr-GAN-choo-uhn)—very large in size or amount

goatee (goh-TEE)—a small beard around the mouth and chin

incessant (in-SES-uhnt)—continuing without interruption

inherently (in-HAIR-uhnt-lee)—being a part of the nature of a person or thing

intertwine (in-ter-TWINE)—to twist or weave together

intervention (in-tur-VEN-shuhn)—the act of taking action in order to help solve a problem

invasion (in-VAY-zhuhn)—the act of entering a place in an attempt to take control of it

legacy (LEG-uh-see)—qualities and actions that one is remembered for

masculine (MAS-kyuh-lin)—of or having to do with men

mundane (muhn-DANE)—ordinary

mustache (muh-STASH)—hair that grows on a person's top lip

netherworld (NETH-er-wurld)—the world of the dead

purge (PURJ)—to clean thoroughly by getting rid of unwanted items

quadrant (KWAHD-ruhnt)—section of an area that is divided into four parts

reunion (ree-YOON-yuhn)—a gathering of two or more people who have not seen each other for a long time

sanity (SAN-ih-tee)—good mental health

sulfurous (suhl-FYOOR-uhs)—of, relating to, or containing the element sulfur

wanton (WON-tuhn)—showing no thought or care for the rights, feelings, or safety of others

VISUAL QUESTIONS & WRITING PROMPTS

1. When Cyborg gets a mustache, the Titans all react differently. How do the words and picture in this panel tell you about the friends' different feelings about the situation?

CYBORG! YOUR FACE!
THIS CHANGES EVERYTHING!
IS IT TRUE, BRO?
GROSS.

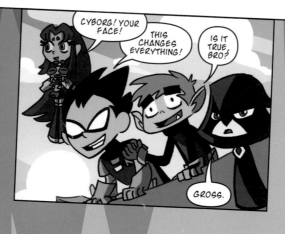

2. How do the creators let you know that Cyborg's mustache is speaking in these panels? What clues do they give you?

DON'T BE SCARED! I'M HERE TO HELP CYBORG RUN HIS LIFE AND BECOME A REAL MAN! I'M GOING TO BE A NEW PART OF YOUR TEAM!
BUT HOW DID YOU GET HERE?
"WHEN CYBORG'S MUSTACHE GREW IN, THE FACIAL HAIR GOT INTERTWINED WITH HIS ARMOR AND PRESTO BINGO...I WAS BORN!"

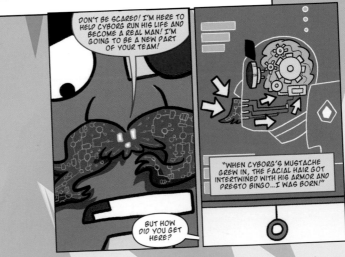

3. Raven mentions "sibling rivalry" in this panel. What do you think this means based on the art and the text?

OH, GREAT. THE "SONS OF TRIGON."
WHAT'S THE MATTER, TWO-EYES? AREN'T YOU HAPPY TO SEE YOUR LOVING BROTHERS?
BACK OFF. I DON'T HAVE TIME FOR SIBLING RIVALRY.

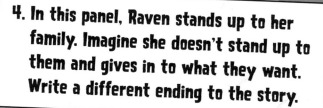

4. In this panel, Raven stands up to her family. Imagine she doesn't stand up to them and gives in to what they want. Write a different ending to the story.

--SO LEAVE ME ALONE!

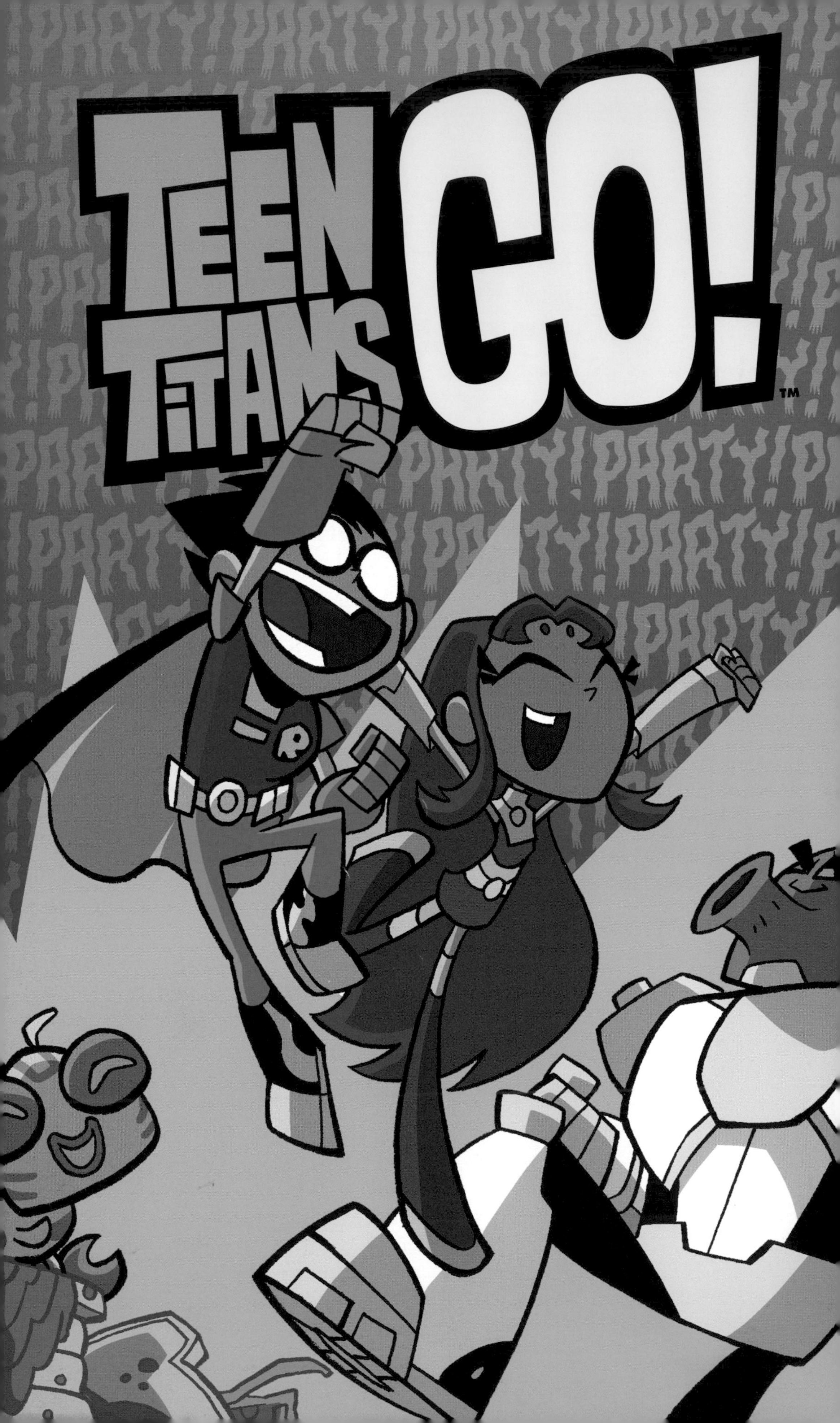
TEEN TITANS GO!™
PARTY! PARTY! PARTY!

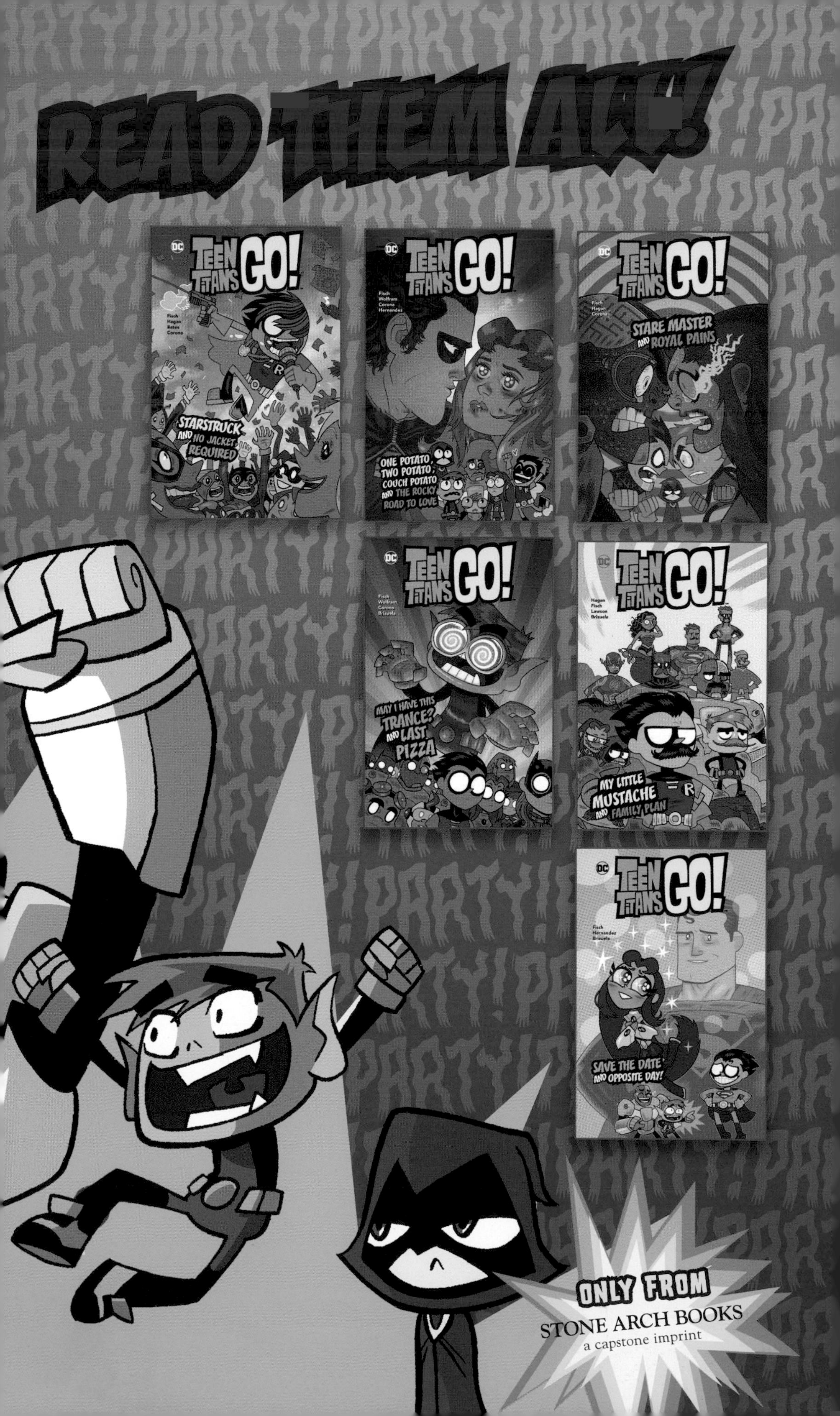
READ THEM ALL!
TEEN TITANS GO!
Fisch Hagan Bates Corona
STARSTRUCK AND NO JACKET REQUIRED
TEEN TITANS GO!
Fisch Wolfram Corona Hernandez
ONE POTATO, TWO POTATO, COUCH POTATO AND THE ROCKY ROAD TO LOVE
TEEN TITANS GO!
Fisch Hagan Corona
STARE MASTER AND ROYAL PAINS
TEEN TITANS GO!
Fisch Wolfram Corona Brizuela
MAY I HAVE THIS TRANCE? AND LAST PIZZA
TEEN TITANS GO!
Hagan Fisch Lawson Brizuela
MY LITTLE MUSTACHE AND FAMILY PLAN
TEEN TITANS GO!
Fisch Hernandez Brizuela
SAVE THE DATE AND OPPOSITE DAY!
ONLY FROM
STONE ARCH BOOKS
a capstone imprint

TEEN TITANS GO!™

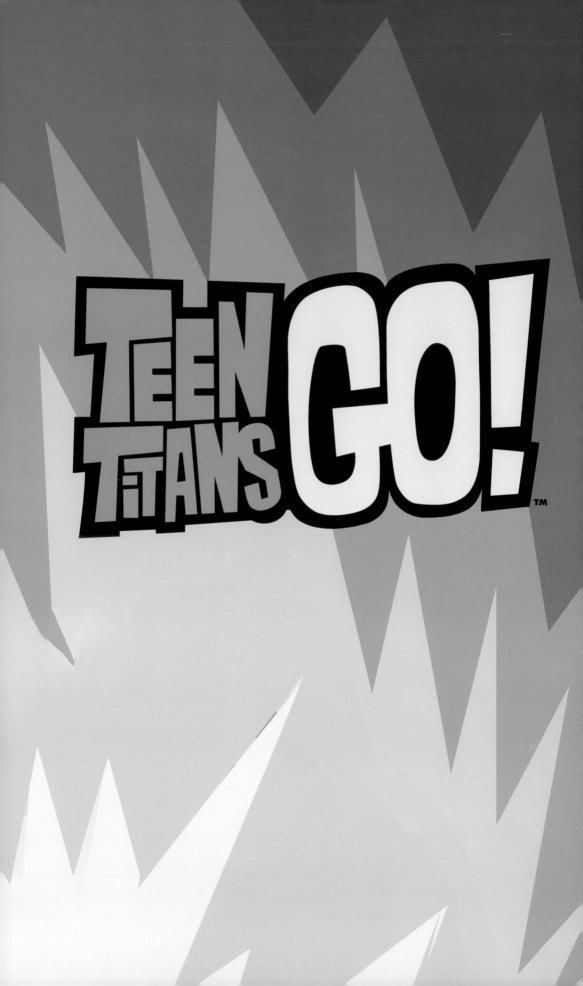